Leap of Faith
&
Other Tales from
The Pennsylvania Coal Region

PENNSYLVANIA HERITAGE BOOKS

An Imprint of University of Scranton Press
Scranton and London

*An imprint in honor of Joseph P. McKerns (1950-2004)*
*of Shenandoah and Mahanoy City;*
*Grandson of Irish and Polish immigrants who worked the*
*Railroads and coal mines of Pennsylvania;*
*Champion of those working men and women*
*who have always been Pennsylvania's greatest heritage.*

# Leap of Faith
# &
# Other Tales from
# The Pennsylvania Coal Region

Richard Benyo

PENNSYLVANIA HERITAGE BOOKS
An Imprint of
UNIVERSITY OF SCRANTON PRESS
Scranton and London

Library of Congress Cataloging-in-Publication Data

Benyo, Richard.
  Leap of faith & other tales from the Pennsylvania coal region / Richard Benyo.
     p. cm.
  ISBN 978-1-58966-185-1 (pbk.)
  1. Benyo, Richard--Childhood and youth. 2. Mauch Chunk (Pa.)--Biography. 3.
Jim Thorpe (Pa.)--Biography. 4. Boys--Pennsylvania--Mauch Chunk--Biography.
5. Boys--Pennsylvania--Jim Thorpe--Biography. 6. Mauch Chunk (Pa.)--Social life
and customs. 7. Jim Thorpe (Pa.)--Social life and customs.  I. Title. II. Title: Leap of
faith and other tales from the Pennsylvania coal region.
  F159.M4B465 2009
  974.8'26--dc22
  [B]

                                                                                  2009021891

Distribution:
UNIVERSITY OF SCRANTON PRESS
Chicago Distribution Center
11030 S. Langley
Chicago, IL  60628

PRINTED IN THE UNITED STATES OF AMERICA

*For*
*RHONDA*
*a story in itself*

# Contents

# Introduction

THESE STORIES are placed in what might seem like the mythical towns of Mauch Chunk and East Mauch Chunk, two rival boroughs occupying opposite sides of the Lehigh River—each side very much distinct from the other. East Mauch Chunk sprawls along an ancient alluvial fan eroded off the flank of Bear Mountain; Mauch Chunk is squished almost claustrophobically between the sides of an intimate little valley.

The Mauch Chunks are anything but mythical, even though technically they no longer exist. I didn't create them as a literary device like Faulkner's Yoknapatawpha County, Mississippi or Tolkien's Middle Earth. The Mauch Chunks actually did exist at one time: two rival towns with completely different styles, each with its own Catholic Church, its own mayor and police force, its own road crews, and its own fiercely loyal citizens.

Like so many other Coal Region towns and cities, the Mauch Chunks were at one time the beneficiaries and later the victims of their rich natural resources.

When coal was discovered in the early 1800s, an avalanche of money flowed to the remote river valley. Business tycoons Josiah White, George Hauto, and Erskine Hazard rushed in to capitalize on the coal that was sorely needed— for burgeoning steel mills in Bethlehem and Philadelphia, and to heat homes downriver. The trio was quickly granted use of all the water that flowed in the Lehigh River so that they could float barges of anthracite coal to eager markets. They constructed the Switchback Railroad, the first gravity railroad in the world, from Summit Hill to Mauch Chunk. Coal from Lansford, Coaldale, and Summit Hill was loaded onto the cars and they were run by gravity to the bottom of Mt. Pisgah. They were then hauled up to the peak by steam power, and the coal was dumped down chutes to be loaded onto the barges that waited along the river's edge.

Railroad magnate Asa Packer built the Lehigh Railroad on the east side of the river to further speed the transport of coal to the hungry maws of steel mills. Packer and numerous other millionaires took up residence in Mauch Chunk, which was spared the ugliness of hard-coal mining because it served only as the shipping point, not the source of the coal. Mauch Chunk became a popular tourist town, second only to Niagara Falls as a honeymoon destination. Because of its location, snuggled amidst close-in mountains, it became known as "The Switzerland of America." At its height, there were nine luxury hotels and a dozen millionaires, and the town was visited by U.S. presidents and celebrities of the stage. Well-known big bands, like the Tommy Dorsey Orchestra, regularly performed through the 1940s.

As coal declined as a prime resource, the Switchback Railroad was converted to an amusement ride, carrying passengers on a breathtaking roller-coaster ride over the eight miles from Summit Hill to the Mauch Chunks and back. Some consider it the first roller coaster in the world.

But by the end of World War II, both coal and railroading had had their day, and the coal towns of central-eastern

Pennsylvania were in sharp decline. The union bosses and the millionaires had long since left Mauch Chunk, the rails began to grow rust, and the laborers who lived in Mauch Chunk began to commute to factory jobs in Hazleton, Palmerton, and Bethlehem. Young people graduated from high school and their first priority was to escape the Mauch Chunks. Seldom did their parents discourage them.

It was into this economic trough that veterans of World War II fell. The glory days of the Coal Region were gone. The railroads barely operated. Hard coal now dribbled out of small, independent mines "up the road" in Coaldale and Lansford. The last coal mine in Lansford (Lanscoal No. 9) closed in May of 1972. At the end it was being operated by a dozen hard-core miners, all of them past retirement age.

The Switchback Railroad had vanished before World War II. The tracks and rolling stock had been sold to the Japanese as scrap metal. The local joke from returning soldiers was that "We got the Switchback back in World War II—at Pearl Harbor—in the form of Japanese bombs."

With the return of the World War II soldiers, the much heralded Baby Boom began in the Mauch Chunks as it did elsewhere in the country. The two parochial grade schools (Immaculate Conception on Broadway in Mauch Chunk and St. Joseph's on Sixth and School Streets in East Mauch Chunk) and the public schools were suddenly bursting at the seams.

It is in this era, the early 1950s, that most of these stories are set. It was an era when the Mauch Chunks were once again in transition. Not just because of the mob of kids running around loose like wild animals, reverting to the primordial as soon as they got out of sight of their parents, but also on the adult front, when the editor and co-publisher of the Mauch Chunk Times News, Joe Boyle, spearheaded a movement (the Nickel-a-Week Program) to raise money to bring industry to the towns.

In a fortuitous coincidence, Jim Thorpe, the famed and then disgraced Indian athlete, died an ignoble death on March 28, 1953 while living in a modest trailer home in Lomita, California. His widow attempted to return his body to his native Oklahoma, where she wanted his Sac and Fox tribes to build a monument under which he could be buried, but his tribe wanted nothing to do with him. She then approached his college alma mater, the Carlisle Indian School in Pennsylvania, but they didn't want him either.

While in Philadelphia attempting to have the body taken under the care of NFL Commissioner Bert Bell, Thorpe's widow saw a television report about the Nickel-a-Week Program in the Mauch Chunks and she suddenly had an idea where Jim Thorpe might be buried, even though he'd never been to Mauch Chunk in his life. The beauty of her plan was that the little town even had an Indian name, so there could be an Indian connection. (Mauch Chunk is Leni Lenape Indian for Bear Mountain, referring to the massive mountain that broods over the towns and that to the Indians resembled a slumbering bear.)

Mrs. Thorpe approached Joe Boyle and his supporters and a movement was mounted to ease the economic burden on the two towns by joining them together so they would need only one mayor, one borough council, one police force, and so on. In 1954, the citizens of Mauch Chunk and East Mauch Chunk voted (barely) to combine and become Jim Thorpe, Pennsylvania.

The change did not immediately bring the prosperity that the citizens had anticipated. For a time the town continued to decline and then gradually, against the naysayers and obstructionists—and there were many—the town reinvented itself into its 1880s image as a tourist Mecca. By the end of the twentieth century, the resurrection had taken place.

Ironically, in the dark days of the '50s, an innovation emerged in the central-eastern Pennsylvania Coal Region that would eventually impact the entire world—for well and ill. In nearby Manahoy City, CATV (Community Antenna Television, a.k.a. cable TV) was invented when appliance-store owners found they could not sell "them new-fangled television sets" if the potential customer could not pull in television signals over the surrounding mountains. The store owners banded together to build a huge common antenna and sold hookups to customers. Jim Thorpe was one of the first towns to benefit from the new service. Now the remote, economically depressed little burg could become a voyeur to what was happening in Philadelphia and New York City, and in so doing, expand its horizons.

Although the Mauch Chunks have not existed since 1954, most of the older folks who lived through it all still think of themselves as "Chunkers." Most of my generation, born after World War II, are suspended between both Chunk and Thorpe. We often referred to our town as Jim Chunk.

Childhood in East Mauch Chunk in the 1950s was not idyllic. Trust me on this. East Mauch Chunk was neither Nirvana nor Shangri La. The towns were gritty; there was no central sewage and no garbage pickup. The trees along the railroad track were stunted from the locomotive exhausts. There were periods when our fathers were out of work for months at a time and we lived on surplus food that was given out once a week at the firehouse on 9th Street. Many of the adult males burned with bitter resentment about how their lives had turned out and not infrequently took their anger out on their kids.

But in their own way, the Mauch Chunks were a decent place to grow up as a kid. In the summer months, kids were gone from breakfast until supper, and then gone again until the streetlights came on. We were digging mines in the side of the mountain, throwing together impromptu ballgames with three kids on a side and a shared catcher, or chasing each other up and over Bear Mountain. People didn't lock their doors. Kids under the tutelage of the Good Nuns were disciplined and generally behaved (or God help them). There were plenty of comic books and baseball cards to trade, we enjoyed an excellent little library on Broadway (if we could avoid getting caught and beaten up on the way there or back by the Irish kids). There were basketball hoops at every schoolyard, and there was so little crime that the cops got fatter and more sedentary as the years went by.

For better or worse, we all own the era and the geography in which we grew up. As each resident of the Mauch Chunks dies, one more light in the tough little town goes out. Eventually the mythical towns of Mauch Chunk and East Mauch Chunk that straddled the dogleg in the Lehigh River where millionaires thrived—and a century later people were destitute and despairing before being revivified—will vanish. The Mauch Chunks will be no more.

Hopefully, some of these stories will help keep a light in the window after all of us Chunkers have left for our just rewards or punishments.

# The Journey

Little Danny found the body on Tuesday afternoon while playing at the river below the Glen Onoko Falls. It had been floating peacefully, face up, in a small cove between the rocks under the railroad bridge where Danny and his best friend, Kurt, spent most of their summer days swimming.

Danny had been going there by himself that week while Kurt was away visiting his father, who "lived somewhere north of here, in a big house," and who Kurt visited every few months. Kurt was to stop at an aunt's for a few days on his way home. Danny was eager for Kurt to return so that he could show him what he'd found.

The body had so fascinated Danny that he hadn't even bothered to go swimming that week. His mother had forbidden him to go swimming alone, and he usually obeyed her on that count, "'cause it just wasn't any fun swimming alone." She had also told him, over and over again, not to play near the river, but that seemed silly to the eight-year-old's mind, especially when he and Kurt had the time of their young lives at the water's edge.

But even had he enjoyed swimming by himself, he wouldn't have even thought of it. His mind was too filled with the novelty of the body; his every thought was absorbed by it.

He had scrambled over the rock slope after climbing down a rusting ladder that descended to the concrete foundations of the bridge on that Tuesday, intending to spend the afternoon tossing rocks at any fish he could catch jumping at flies that buzzed above the water in the shade of the trestle. His eyes had been downcast, on the rubble, to make sure that the balls of his sneakers landed only on solid rocks, and had not caught sight of the cove until he scratched to a stop on the huge rock overhanging the water.

At first he thought that there was some rubbish there, floating on the water, that had come down the river—old rags and wood chips that collected in the cove and that Kurt used to curse at, before cleaning it up. "If ya hit any a' that stuff when ya dive in, you'll split a skull," he used to say, as he'd spin the oversized gold ring on his thumb. He had a habit of doing that. His father had given him the gold ring, and Danny would give it a spin every time he said something that he was completely sure of.

He lowered himself to his haunches atop the rock and stared at the body for some minutes, not a muscle on his young body making even a quiver. His entire being was absorbed in what he saw.

If ya hit any a' that stuff when ya dive in, you'll split a skull. Kurt always said things like grownups would. Maybe because he was a year older than Danny and knew more because he had been a lot of places that Danny had never seen and some places he'd never even heard of. Kurt was a real prince of a guy as far as Danny could tell, and Danny took no pains to hide his admiration or his acknowledgment of Kurt's station. That was just how things were supposed to be. His parents had told him more than once that the older a fellow was the more he knew. That was only right. Older meant you'd been around more—seen more stuff.

He began to shift between the heels and balls of his shoes, rocking back and forth awkwardly, uncertainly, glancing about curiously, and becoming aware of the sweat that gathered in his sneakers, making his socks very uncomfortable. Reaching into his back pocket, he took out the freshly folded handkerchief, which he never found it necessary to use, and ran it across his brow like his father did on a humid day when the flies near the house were attracted to him.

His lips opened and just as quickly closed.

Maybe the man would holler at him for being where he knew he wasn't supposed to be.

"Hi ya," he breathed, not loud enough for even his own ears to hear. "Hello," he said, louder. "You sure float good, mister."

The man stared up at the trestle, far overhead, with his glazy, vague eyes, as though he recognized one of the names written on the ironwork and was remembering something about that person—something worthy of very special attention.

"You float real good," Danny repeated, shifting his weight. "But you sure give a guy the willies by not lookin' at him," he added to himself.

Danny wasn't really too bothered about the man ignoring him. Everyone else seemed to ignore him, too, until he did something that was supposed to be wrong. At times like that he got undivided attention, usually from his mother, who told him how bad he'd grow up to be "if you don't mend your ways." His father, when he was home, didn't much bother him one way or the other.

His father had taken him for a walk up Robinson's Creek one time after church last summer. Danny had been on walks up Robinson's Creek with Kurt, but it never seemed to be quite the same territory when he traveled it with an adult. Danny went to church every week with the Snyders from Lazy Acres Farm. His parents thought it would make him "grow up right." He didn't understand how sitting in a stuffy room listening to a stuffy preacher talk about things he didn't even understand was going to help him to be "right" when he grew up.

"I went to church this week," Danny said to the man in the water, and then wondered why he had said it. "But I didn't really want to go," he added anyway. He idly fingered a smoothed rock beside his shoe, not sure whether he should pretend to ignore the man as he was being ignored, or whether he should try again to get his attention.

"Hey mister!" he yelled. "Why are you swimmin' with your clothes on?" He remembered the time he'd been crossing the fishing creek down behind his house and had slipped on the green slime that covered the rocks. He'd gotten his clothes all wet, and—even through the memory of the spanking he'd gotten—he could recall the sluggish weight of the damp flannel shirt and the blue jeans clinging to him. It didn't seem like the way to swim.

"You got a shirt like Mr. Huzzleman's got," he called. He noticed that there was a rip in the man's pant leg and a growth of beard on his face. Men around there didn't wear beards.

"You a bum?" he asked, quickly throwing his hand over his mouth. Mr. Huzzleman had told him that, and Mr. Huzzleman knew. He lived a couple of miles downriver, in a little house by the water's edge, under the overhang of the

Lower Glen Cliff. Danny wanted to be like Mr. Huzzleman someday. He didn't do anything but live in his little weathered house and take walks with his dog Mutt. He took trips sometimes, too, and never got bothered by people, because his only visitors came when he wasn't home. Danny didn't know what to do to cover up his improper question, so he got up and paced leisurely around on the overhang, a few pebbles in his hand.

He looked at the man's hair, all wet and plastered-back looking, and thought that it looked a lot like the pastor's on a hot summer morning when he really got excited about something and started raising his voice. He wondered absently, as he passed the pebbles, one by one, from hand to hand, why the pastor always told the people who came to listen to him that they should have patience with their fellow man—and how impatient he got when the O'Donnell triplets cried while he was talking. Danny sometimes felt like crying at times like that, when he was sore from sitting still so long and old Mrs. Helferty, who always managed to sit behind him, started hissing to him when he squirmed to get a new position on life and feel a little better off for his suffering.

A fish jumped and Danny automatically sailed a pebble at it. It overshot the bulls-eye of the fish's ripple, skipped once, and clattered onto the bridge support's flat foundation.

The man in the water didn't move.

Danny looked at him with a half-cocked head, the shadow of doubt stealing across his tanned face.

"Mister," he called. "Are you for real?" (He liked that question. His cousin from the city always used it. It sounded big-time.) He had his muscles tensed, prepared to react to any movement from the man. He was always afraid of asking a grown-up a face-to-face question. For some reason it always seemed to get them cross at him.

No reaction came, and he was half-confident of his own judgment. He tossed another rock over the quiet body, this one splashing somewhat closer to it than the last one. He watched as the ripples from it spread, gently rocking the body as they reached it.

He sighed aloud. "You aren't real. You aren't a real man at all."

Swinging into a standing position, the rocks still clutched in his hands, Danny climbed down the overhang to the water's edge, where he paused to look at the body from a new angle. Humming to himself, he threw a rock at the body. It sailed over the head, skipped once and sank. He threw another. It hit the chest with a soft-sounding plop and bounced off to the other side.

The man didn't move; some ripples sailed away from the body and Danny watched them lap the shore at his feet. He absently dropped a rock into the last three.

He looked out to the raging rapids beyond the little cove, and then at the quiet body on the quiet pool, and thought of how the river flowed on so swiftly, completely bypassing the body and the pool, the way the Turnpike passed Mauch Chunk at 65 miles per hour a few miles away, while in the town no one even thought of going that fast—except late at night when the teenagers with hot cars raced up and down North Street. "You're away from the rapids," he said, half-aloud. "You're part of it but your place isn't there."

He tossed another rock, surely, deliberately, at the opposite bank; it fell short—far short.

After a moment he tried, by pulling water toward him, to move the body to shore. A few minutes showed him that this was futile. So, taking off his shoes and trousers, he waded out, feeling the cold water up his legs and the sand and pebbles between his toes. He involuntarily shivered as the water rose to his belly, and he moved toward the irregular patches of sunlight that checkered the water. It gave him a little warmth to counter the cold of the pool.

The dull green, sudsy water was to his chest by the time his hand touched the damp sleeve of the body. He moved slowly, a little more seriously than he did while retrieving a log that had invaded their pool, hoping half-heartedly that the body might well be a store-window dummy from one of the big towns that his father told him were behind the mountains, upriver—towns with funnier names than Ruddles' Run and Mauch Chunk.

He knew—or at least he thought he knew—that dummies were hard and that this one wasn't. It was more like his Grampa Steve had been the morning he'd found him sleeping behind the shed near the house. He'd never seen him after that, but he remembered how softly tense his grampa's arm had been when he had shaken him.

Reaching the shore again, he shivered anew, and struggled to get the rough sand from his feet so that it wouldn't bother him when he put his shoes on. He had left the body near shore, one arm on dry land; he felt that he had properly beached it for the time being.

He knew, though, that if one of the big towns upriver opened one of their dams like they sometimes did, the body would float out of the cove and into the river's current. Once it got into the current it would be lost. Some of the railroad

men downstream would fish it out like they did Kurt's raft
the time he had forgotten to tie it up overnight.

Remembering the mooring cable from their raft, he
searched about for it, finding it under the rock where they
had hidden it. It was a frayed piece of rope, knotted, mold-
ing, and spliced in several places with other pieces of rope not
of the same thickness. They had found the pieces on some of
their trips around the dump behind East Mauch Chunk.

Danny scampered down the rocks and put the loop
around the wrist that lay upon the smooth rocks of the shore.
He took the other end toward a gnarled tree where they
sometimes dried their clothes. The rope didn't quite reach,
so he went and moved the body a few feet upstream, in line
with the tree.

"Boy, you're heavy," he said as he struggled with the un-
gainly weight. "How come you didn't hold back so much
when I pulled you to shore? Huh?" He didn't expect an answer anymore.

He moved down to the tree, the end of the rope clutched
in his one hand, the other hand clenched but empty. He fas-
tened the rope as securely as he knew how, glancing more
than once at the body lying half in and half out of the water. He imagined that he saw waves of steam rising from the
damp chest as the rays of the sun fell across the thick shirt.

Standing over the body again, he got a strange feeling
as he gazed and traced the contours of the face—wanting to
touch it to know it better, but afraid of how he might feel.

Danny swallowed once, twice, a third time, and rose,
making his way up the slope to climb the rusty ladder and
head back home so that he could beat the sun to the horizon
and not miss his supper.

He came back the next day to check on the body but did not stay around too long. He was eager for Kurt to get back and see it, and he had begun to feel uneasy around it.

The body floated peacefully that night as it had the night before, a few animals nosing the fingertips but none prepared to bother with it once they had satisfied their curiosity.

Friday was half-spent when stones began to clatter off the bulwark of concrete foundations as two sets of sneakered feet disturbed the calls of the kingfisher. Danny came down the ladder first, followed by a slightly larger edition of himself with unruly black hair and a sleeveless shirt.

"You better not of brung me out here on my first day back for nothin'," he called to Danny, who was too excited about showing his find to his friend to listen to anything except the laudatory comments that he knew would come when Kurt saw it.

Danny led him to the tree. Kurt, seeing the rope, followed it to the water's edge—to where it ended in a knot on the body's wrist.

His eyes grew wide, his face pale, and the corners of his mouth dropped.

"What's ya think of my body, huh, Kurt?" Danny asked, smiling proudly, unsurely, waiting for Kurt's reaction.

Kurt did not move for some minutes as the two of them stood like carved statues by the water, Kurt affected by what he saw of the body, Danny transfixed by the expression that began to grow—too slowly for Danny to follow—on Kurt's face.

Neither spoke, and strangely enough no animal's voice

filled the void. The only sound was the slight lap-lap of the water splattering itself heedlessly on the shore.

Danny's stare of surprise and confusion became one of fear as he watched his friend's eyes become glassy and saw the muscles of his neck begin to move sluggishly, as though he were in the water himself, with something caught in his throat that he was trying to swallow—so that he could breathe.

The first sob that escaped Kurt's lips made Danny jump from his stupor. He stumbled backwards in his surprise, his foot catching on the cold hand tied to the shore—sending him sprawling. He felt sick in the pit of his stomach as he struggled to his feet and saw Kurt running up the slope.

Danny stood stunned as he watched Kurt sit down on the top of the rock slope, his head between his knees, his body moving in quick jerks. He saw him bring his hands to his face, saw them twitching and moving, and then saw Kurt let them fall to his sides.

He wanted to yell something to Kurt, but he didn't know what. Turning with a questioning look at the body, Danny felt alone. He shivered as he had when the river's cold water played on his belly.

He stood motionless for a long time: long enough to see Kurt rise, a stone in his hand and a sob heaving his shoulders. Danny saw him fling the stone out at the river with a curse that Danny did not understand. But he watched, fascinated, as the stone rose in an arc over the pool, over the rapids, and fell with a crack among the rocks on the other side.

By the time he turned back, Kurt was gone. "Wait for me!" he called after him. There was no answer.

He turned, walked to the gnarled tree, unfastened the mooring cable and carried it to the water's edge, where he placed it on the body's chest. It took some effort to shove the body away from the shore, but he managed to do it. He left the rope where it was; it would do Danny no good anymore.

Then he climbed to where Kurt had stood and was taken aback by the smell that met him. He turned, bewildered and afraid, toward the ladder, and saw a glint on the stone. He snatched at it on the run. And, as his fingers recognized the form of Kurt's ring, he looked at the body in time to see it leave the cove and enter the current, still very peaceful, but no longer important. It was gone for him as Kurt's ring was gone. It just was of no use anymore.

Danny dropped the ring where he had found it and turned to go.

He knew that Kurt would never come back to their pool, and he knew that his mother forbad him to go swimming alone. It wasn't any fun to do things alone, anyway.

He watched the body slowly reach the swift, white-foamed water, saw it get tugged into the swells and peaks and bob up and down as it was carried away, the rope falling into the water, trailing after it.

As he reached the ladder, he spooked out a brown bat. It flapped out on its leathery wings and almost instantly stopped in midair under the trestlework, caught in a mass of spider webs. It struggled, lashing out violently, until its weight broke the threads. It fell, unable to disengage its wings, into the cold water below.

*Originally published in The Dipple Chronicle, July/September 1971.*

# Leap of Faith

It was most likely that the tons of stripped-out, stirred-up anthracite coal dust hauled through town on trains and barges and frittered away on the wind had created a mutant function in the chromosomes of family men on the lowest two blocks of Spruce Street in East Mauch Chunk. Between 1944 and 1948, fourteen children were born to these men: one extremely feminine girl named Betsy O'Connell, whom everyone adored because she was unique and 100% authentically nice; a full dozen boys of varying sizes, shapes, and temperaments; and one tomboy named Henrietta Zenko—who demanded to be called Hank and who was the co-honcho of the wannabe infamous Spruce Street Gang.

Or perhaps it was psychologically induced into the sperm by the remoteness of the lower two blocks of Spruce Street from the rest of town. Below was a very steep park that emptied into River Street and from there to the Lehigh River. Above, a ravine that separated them from Bear Mountain. Folks used the ravine as a dump, and it was overrun by rats the size of lunch boxes. Some studies suggest that a male's psychological state at the time of conception can determine the sex of his offspring. Who knows what kind of stresses assailed grizzled miners and railroad workers who, after a meal and a few bottles of beer carried garbage down through their backyards only to be confronted by a phalanx of glowing-red rodent eyes? Spruce Street fathers never broached the subject of rats and were the only adult men in town who ever had a kind thing to say about cats.

Once the transportation of coal ceased, the proportion of male to female births gradually normalized. But whatever the cause, this proliferation of boys over girls was unique to Spruce Street. In fact, in the rest of East Mauch Chunk, the ratio was slightly in favor of girls.

There is less ready information about the male/female mix in Mauch Chunk proper, brooding over there on the other side of the Lehigh River. That was enemy territory, and the very reason in the first place for the existence of the Spruce Street Gang—and of the North Street Gang, the Front Street Gang, the Bear Mountain Hillers, and the Up-towners.

While East Mauch Chunk sprawled up the side of an ancient alluvial fan, Mauch Chunk proper clung precarious-ly to steep mountains. While East Mauch Chunk was inhab-ited primarily by Germans, Poles, and Slavs, Mauch Chunk proper was overrun by Irish. Several Irish families did live quite peacefully in East Mauch Chunk, but they were East Chunkers first and foremost. Betsy O'Connell was "one of us," even though her family went to the Irish Catholic Church in Mauch Chunk instead of the German Catholic Church in East Mauch Chunk. Even later, when she attend-ed the Catholic high school across town, she remained "one of us," now and forever, a homegrown product.

There was one boy on Spruce Street, however, who flirt-ed with not being "one of us," even though he was born among us as surely as Betsy: an only child named Eugene Likuzina. He only rarely spent time with the kids on lower Spruce Street, and perhaps because of that he had acquired the nickname You. Not Hugh or Yew or Hew or Hue, and not Gene, but You. As in "Hey, You!" or "Yeah, I'm talkin' ta You!" Eugene hated his given name, but it was the Catholic way—to name children after long-dead saints. And Catholic saints usually became saints because they were martyred. (Eugene Likuzina harbored a theory that they got themselves martyred because their parents gave them such dreadful names.)

Eugene Likuzina flirted with not being "one of us" because he kept pretty much to himself. His mother loved and spoiled him as her one and only child; his father blamed You's very existence as the reason he would have no more children. Eugene's mother underwent a hysterectomy following his birth, which Mrs. Likuzina determined was due to childbirth "warping" her "plumbing." Mr. Likuzina said it was Eugene that was warped, and giving birth to that inherent warpiness had destroyed his wife's "baby maker." From the father's constant condemnation, Eugene had developed a stutter. Between this and being a "Momma's boy," Eugene spent much of his time alone, either reading in his room or at the town library, or furtively wandering the slopes of Bear Mountain.

He was as skittish as a deer and as secretive as a wolf. He knew every stone on Bear Mountain. And when his world became unbearable, he would run from the back of his house, down the narrow path through the dump to the lumberyard at the bottom of the ravine, across a wooden plank over the septic creek, and up the mountain to its peak. He leaped from boulder to boulder, and plunged over the far side, surfing steep waves of rock. He then raced around the base of the mountain along the railroad tracks and back home, the exercise effectively defusing him. In his compulsive way, Eugene kept on graph paper a meticulous record of his elapsed times up and over and around the mountain.

The vigorous running served him well. When the Spruce Street Gang could find nothing else on which to vent their spleen and "You" Likuzina wandered into view, he easily outran them. He even made short shrift of the Mararsko twins, two eager hounds his age and the fastest the gang had to offer.

The stars and planets must have aligned in a very outrageous manner in the summer of 1957, because the Spruce Street Gang actually invited You Likuzina to join their gang, and You actually agreed to do just that.

Why the Spruce Street Gang suddenly wanted You as a member instead of as a victim remains uncertain. Perhaps they were tired of chasing him, and wanted to punish him in some other, more perverse way. Certainly the initiation they planned for him points to that possibility.

Why You agreed to go through the initiation is quite clear. On his way home from the town library in Mauch Chunk one Saturday night, three Irish Catholics from one of the gangs over there had jumped him. They punched him in the stomach, knocking the air out of him, stole his library books, and pushed him down a bank of ashes, ripping his polo shirt. The payment for the library books came out of his allowance, and You read five or six books a week, so a week's worth of books really hammered the shit out of his nest egg. He regarded the invitation to go through the annual August initiation as a means of securing protection from further embarrassment and fiscal distress.

Although the Spruce Street Gang generally had no more

creativity than did other gangs, the same cannot be said for their initiation ritual. Kids on both sides of the river revered its protocol. Initiations were held only during the month of August, performed one per day for as long as it took to bring in or freeze out the applicants. Each initiation was customized to the victim, and some had become the stuff of legends.

The executive council designed initiations. The council consisted of the two oldest gang members, Henrietta . . . er . . . Hank Zenko and Curly Horinski, as well as the council's traveling secretary, Barney "The Weasel" Keller/Rift.

Hank was a slightly built but wiry female with short hair and perpetually skinned knuckles who took exception to being referred to as a female but was gradually losing the battle to puberty. In the animal world, she'd have been a cat.

Curly was bear-like, thick-muscled, and thick-witted, with an unpredictable temper and—when riled—astonishing speed for his bulk. He favored pompadoured hair held in check by what appeared to be 10W-40 crankcase oil, wore a black leather jacket with more studs than a snow tire, carried a pocketknife in every pocket and a switchblade in his right boot, and occasionally entertained himself by working on an India-ink tattoo on the back of his right hand. It was supposed to be a skull and crossbones, but it looked more like a map of Africa. His father had died five years before and Curly was indulged by his mother, who'd had him late in life. In two years, he'd be sixteen and attempt to restart his father's '44 Buick, which slouched on cinder blocks in the backyard of their double-house. He frequently sat behind the steering wheel, and sometimes invited a lucky gang member to ride shotgun to nowhere.

Barney "The Weasel" Keeler/Rift (with a slash, not a hyphen) only lived in East Mauch Chunk during the summers, paroled to his grandmother's care. He sported two last names because his mother was divorced—the only divorced woman any of the kids on Spruce Street knew. Keller was her name, Rift her ex-husband's. Built like Hank (but without the slightly budding breasts), The Weasel had wild black hair, the pallor of a corpse, and had been born with a cigarette butt dangling from his lower lip. For all the cigarettes he'd smoked—and they were sufficient to turn his fingers sunflower yellow—he'd never paid for one. He shoplifted cigarettes—not by the pack, but by the carton.

The cigarettes may have been related to his pyromaniac tendencies, which had resulted the previous year in the scorching of the makeshift baseball diamond in MacGregor's lot. His grandmother claimed that Barney was at home with her making lemonade that morning. She was known to come after kids with a broom who had threatened The Weasel. Her broom was on call full time.

These three orchestrated You's initiation on a particularly hot and muggy August afternoon. As arranged, the trio met You at the corner of Third and Spruce. Almost immediately there was a hint of trouble.

"Where the hell's The Stuff?" The Weasel demanded, raising his hand to launch a whack at You, which You, already wired by the prospects of the initiation and ready to flee in his deer-like manner, anticipated and dodged.

"Da-da-down the wa-wa-woods," You stuttered, his head tucked in like a fighter whose defensive skills are finely honed—as indeed they were, from regular cuffs administered by his father.

The Stuff was the first part of the initiation. Although the main element of the initiation was the victim-specific Task, the first part was standardized, a mere formality to determine if the initiate was worthy of consideration. It consisted of the initiate providing the larder for the council: beer, cigarettes, and cookies. Preferably stolen, but gotten any way that worked. The Stuff had better be there—or else.

"You do wanna get let into the Spruce Streeters?" Curly asked, making a muscle with his huge right arm.

"Yeah, yeah," You said, increasingly unsure. "It-it's down here," he said, turning to lead the three down the embankment toward the lumberyard.

"You don't lead us nowhere," Hank said, grabbing You's shirt collar and stopping him in his tracks. "We lead you. Get it?"

"We lead You," The Weasel said. "Get it? We lead You." He coughed around his Lucky Strike.

You dutifully took his place at the back as they dug in their heels and let gravity surf them down toward the sprawling lumberyard at the bottom of the ravine. They reached the lumberyard's fence then turned left and upstream toward the end of the yard where a plank crossed the septic creek.

"Where you got it hidden?" Curly growled as he fell farther behind the other two.

"Across the ca-ca-creek," You said, plodding along behind Curly.

"You ever seen a tattoo like this?" Curly asked, holding his hand above his head as they walked along the narrow path.

"Na-no," You answered. "It's ba-ba-big."

"Damn right it is. An' it ain't even done yet."

Hank and The Weasel were across the plank, arguing about something, when Curly and You arrived. "Okay," Curly said, ignoring the other two, "where's it at?"

You lowered himself over the side of the plank until he stood on a rock that jutted out from the creek bank, reached up under the plank, and began handing paper bags to Curly, who passed them to the others. First came a sack with five bottles of Ballantine beer You had managed to borrow from his mother's German father, who years before had taught him to drink, and—under penalty of death—to keep the fact from You's mother. Then came a penny candy bag with two packs of unfiltered Camels You had paid another kid at school to get for him. Then came a bag with three big packages of sugar cookies that had been on sale at the Acme market.

Curly immediately broke into the cookies and began eating, while The Weasel expertly swirled the cellophane off a pack of Camels and lit one off the Lucky Strike that had burned down to his lower lip. Hank held the beers close to her chest as if she were breast-feeding them.

"Let's go," Hank said, leading the way across the railroad spur line that ran to the lumberyard. The four crossed a little dirt road and pushed through some overhanging mountain laurels to a hidden path. The long, stiff, dark green leaves beat against them.

The trail was familiar to You, as was everything on Bear Mountain from peak to base. He walked as if on a death march, the smoke from The Weasel's Camel wafting back like school-bus exhaust. He realized that the council had mistakenly placed him at the end of the line, which allowed him to run for it if he decided to. Doing just that did cross his mind as the laurel branches came whacking back at him.

The trail went upwards gradually. Bugs buzzed among the bushes, and discovered the perspiring Curly as he moved past. He swatted at them as they feasted on his sweat. Curly wore his trademark black leather jacket no matter what the weather.

To the right, You could see the huge roof of the lumberyard. The thick wet air muffled the sound of men moving about heavily and loading lumber inside the yard. The boards banging against each other sounded like miniature thunderclaps. You could hear the labored breathing of Curly in the lead, the clinking beer bottles that Hank still clutched to her chest, and the swish swish swish whack of the disturbed laurel branches. Somewhere far away, a train whistle bleared tiredly. You's armpits were wet; an occasional drop of sweat slid down his sides, causing a momentary chill.

The path rose forty feet along a cliff that overlooked the rails, the dirt road, and the lumberyard. Behind the lumberyard office were a half-dozen open-ended, roofless cinderblock enclosures that held gravel and sand. Half faced the office; the other half faced the rails. Occasionally, gondola cars delivered loads of gravel or sand, dumping it alongside the tracks where it waited for the front-end-loader operator to get around to moving it into the bins. A white pile of sand sprawled like a miniature dune beside the far side of the tracks.

As they carefully made their way along the cliff face, the laurel bushes that clung to the edge thinned out. Around Curly's wide back, and through The Weasel's smoke screen, You saw the rest of the Spruce Street Gang sprawled on a rocky overhang. You knew the spot well. He'd spent many a summer day there, reading a book and eating a lunch his mother had made for him. High above them was the back-yard of his house. His mother would walk down the back-yard as suppertime approached and call to him to come get washed up and ready for supper. He glanced up. Today the safe boundary of his backyard seemed miles away, almost on another planet.

His attention was pulled back to the lounging Spruce Street Gang, who had come out of their slow-rolling con-versation when they'd noticed the approach of their leaders. There was a general yelping and scurrying as the half-doz-en reclining boys got their feet under them. The Mazarsko twins slunk forward, their eyes taking in everything. The twins were spring-loaded, as though hoping You would make a break for it so they could try one more time to catch him. "Hey, Likuzina," one of them said, "how they hangin'?"

You shrugged.

Filthy Blaski made a grab for a handful of cookies and Curly swatted him. "Fer council members only," Curly growled as he lowered himself onto the rock Filthy had been occupying. Filthy turned toward Hank. "What ya got fer us?" he asked, sniffing around her.

"Nothin' for you," she said, gently setting down the clang-ing bottles on the flat rock that overlooked the lumberyard office. She sat down next to them and stared at the office.

Filthy turned to The Weasel. "Gimme a cig," he whined.

"Gimme a cig," The Weasel whined back. "Get your own cig." He stood against a tree and ignored Filthy, who looked for someone else to bother.

"Hey, Likuzina, ya fairy," he said.

The Weasel's hand shot out and slapped Filthy on the back of the head. "Watch yer mouth. Likuzina may be one of us soon, and when he is, I'm gonna have him beat the livin' shit outta ya just fer funnies."

Filthy stuffed his hands deep in his pockets and wandered off to the edge of the clearing, found a patch of moss, and dropped onto it, pouting.

Three other guys, little Pub Walenski and the Muskowitcz brothers—Nat and Seb—didn't make any move to welcome You or to pick on him. They stood where they'd been sitting, unsure what to do next. Curly pulled out a handful of cookies and tossed them at the three. Filthy came off his moss like a shot to grab his share. The Weasel snorted around his Camel. "Assholes."

Curly, still eating cookies, but now examining each one before he devoured it, waved his tattooed right hand and patted the rock next to him. You wasn't certain the signal was directed at him but inched forward anyway. "Yeah, yeah," Curly said. "Come over here en sit down next to me," he said, making a symbolic move to the left to clear an imaginary space. You sat next to Curly, and Curly wrapped his big arm around You's skinny shoulders. You was enveloped by the aroma of Curly's perspiration.

He sensed rather than saw the rest of the gang inch forward to be part of what was to come next. Some thought back to their own initiations, the memories of which were distorted by the stress they'd been under.

"I like you," Curly said, the sugar from the cookies tapping into a seldom-plumbed well of generosity. "We all like you. You're a little weird, but hey, we're all a little weird, or we wouldn't be on this stupid earth, would we?" You had lived on Spruce Street all of his life and had known Curly— sort of—all of his life, and he'd never heard him talk like this before. It made You more nervous than if Curly'd been his usual blustering self.

"Everyone needs a challenge in life," he continued, "and I know this is the one that's right for you."

"You," someone said from behind them, and laughed. "You. Get it?"

It was The Weasel. You heard the church key grating against the bottle cap of one of the beers; there was a pop and then the sound of Hank taking a long, slow swig.

Curly moved to get into a more comfortable position. "I know you want to be a member of the Spruce Streeters. You desperately want to." Curly laughed. "You need to become one of us. You need to," Curly said, "for your own good."

Someone behind threw a rock through the sparse trees. It arched over the cliff and vanished below onto the tracks. Curly growled.

"You really want to be with us, don'tcha?" Curly asked, squeezing You closer.

"Y-y-y-y-y-yeah, I sure da-da-do," You got out. Someone behind them twittered like a bird.

"Ya did good on getting us The Stuff," Curly said, again squeezing You. "Ya wanna cookie?"

You shook his head. The lumberyard foreman yelled something at one of the workers and the worker yelled back, but they were at the far end of the yard, and You couldn't make out anything but the word "soon."

"All you gotta do ta be in the gang is walk down to that ledge there"—Curly used his free left arm to take in the cliff

edge—"and jump off it inta the sand pile across the way."
Someone behind him laughed uneasily.

"We'll send the pieces home ta yer mommy—if we find
'em all," The Weasel muttered to himself. But by this time
You's senses were keened enough to hear every word for
miles.

"Let's see ya run yer way outta this one," one of the Mazarsko twins whispered.

"That's all ya gotta do, en you're one of us," Curly continued. "You do wanna be one of us, right?"

You shook his head. "Yeah," he said, wondering if this
was better than getting beaten up occasionally by the Irish
Catholics on the way to and from the library. To reach the
sand pile, he'd have to jump a dozen feet out from the overhang and then fall another forty feet. He tried to calculate
quickly the highest place he'd ever jumped from. It couldn't
have been more than a dozen feet.

There was twittering behind him, but he didn't turn. He
hoped that Curly didn't notice the two huge drops of sweat
that escaped his armpits. "You've got all afternoon ta do it,"
Curly explained. "If ya do it before yer mudder comes out in
the backyard  en yells fer ya ta come home fer supper, yer in.
That's it," Curly said. "That's all there is to it."

Curly removed his arm and You realized that he was dis-
missed. "That's all there is," The Weasel said from within a cloud of Camel smoke. "Sucker," he hissed under his
breath.

You pushed himself up from the rock. His limbs felt
as though they belonged to someone else. They were stiff
and uncertain. He glanced only a bit from side to side,
half-consciously catching sight of some of the gang sitting in

the clearing, expressions on their faces that he could not afford the time to fathom. The overhang was bare on top and stood out several feet from the cliff face. He stood safely back and looked over the edge.

The pile of white sand, at least six feet high and a dozen across, was so far away that it looked as though it had been poured from a thimble. Between the cliff and the sand, the hard lines of parallel railroad tracks yawned like a smirking mouth waiting to devour him.

Time slipped a gear. He tried to calculate the geometry of the jump, but his book learning didn't seem to want to kick in today. The hot, humid air suddenly seemed oppressive. He wished he'd never gotten the bright idea of joining the gang. He wished there were a good way, an honorable way, to get out of this. He almost wished his mother would come to the back of the yard and call for him to come home. At the same time, he knew he would die if she did.

The sounds of the gang behind him filtered through. They were here for the duration, guaranteed of getting a good show whether he jumped or not. With the undercurrent of conversation and cutting up behind him, he managed to pick up one of the Mazarsko brothers: "I wouldn't do it, would you? You'd have to be nuts." Someone else came back, "Nobody's ever done it, en nobody's ever gonna do it. So why're we wastin' our time here with Likuzina?"

You took a tentative step onto the overhang. He'd sometimes sat out on the edge while he read a book, but today, in its new role as the connection between where he'd been and where the guys wanted him to be, the place was alien to him.

A lazy fly buzzed past, probably homing in on Curly's sweat.

You turned slowly. The gang was sprawled out on the little clearing like an army between battles. They studiously ignored him, as though he were a leper or a ghost. He tried to catch the eyes of one or the other of them, but they were energetically not looking his way. Except for The Weasel, who regarded him with the generous contempt that he lavished on the world in general.

You walked back into the clearing a few steps and glanced around again. Hank was on her second bottle of warm beer. She sort of looked at him from under unconcerned, lidded eyes. She is like a cat, You thought. He remembered many years back when she'd come around to the house and offered to babysit for him. His mother was kind to her, but explained that Eugene was a precious little thing, and she couldn't entrust him to the protection of anyone else. Henrietta did not hide her disappointment well. A day later, a rock broke one of their back windows.

When he glanced down at Filthy, the guy's usual pleading-for-attention face was downcast, as though he'd be the one to get dumped on when You killed himself, the one volunteered to clean up the pieces of Eugene Likuzina when he landed, Kerplunk, on the railroad tracks. Poor Filthy—a victim's victim.

You wandered a few more yards up the hillside, found an open space, turned and sat down, seemingly studying the rooftop of the lumberyard office. Actually, he stared into space and saw nothing but his own desperate foolishness.

He felt his stomach turn over as he remembered the Irish Catholic kid who'd punched him right under the breastbone. He heard the rush of air and felt the constriction of his chest. He'd hung a hair's breadth from death, the way it feels when you're sick and vomiting into the toilet, as though your hold on life has been wrested by someone else and you're a helpless puppet clinging desperately to a porcelain stranger.

The memory of the assault was too vivid to deny. At least he'd have control over jumping, he told himself. And maybe he wouldn't die or get crippled. Then he wouldn't have to worry about doing this again. For a brief moment he wondered how it would feel when the time came for one of the younger kids to be initiated into the gang. Could he sit by and watch the kid do something like this—something that nobody had ever done?

Do you really want to belong to the gang? You asked himself. Do you really want to belong?

He looked around at the other kids from the neighborhood. Almost everyone he knew was there. Al Kochkie was away with his family on vacation in New Jersey and Bob Simpleski was in summer school—again. But everyone else was right there.

You pushed himself off the ground. The movement brought a momentary silence to the gang—anticipation that this might be it. You walked back to the ledge and forced himself out to the very edge. He looked down to the tracks below. Beyond, the pile of sand, as small as salt spilled on the dining room table. He understood that this was one of those summer afternoons, when clocks run slower, that could go on forever. He heard The Weasel say something to Hank about ". . . never . . . ."

Yes, yes! He said to himself.

He looked down one more time, turned, and marched deliberately up the little hillside. Thick silence filled the clearing. With a short intake of air, You turned and ran toward the overhanging rock. The force of his passing pulled the others off the ground and toward the cliff with him.

He did not feel his legs moving, but he felt the sound of the trees moving past him. He saw the overhang approaching him and the sudden panorama of the ravine, the lumberyard office, the sand and gravel pits, the little spill of sand that was his target, the railroad tracks going off for a million miles in either direction. And then he pushed off and closed his eyes.

He felt peaceful within the blackness, and it seemed to go on for a long time.

For an instant, he pictured his legs being mangled and his body exploding as it hit the railroad ties. But that image was jarred from him as his feet sliced into the fine-grain sand. His legs forced toward his chest as they shared the impact with the forgiving sand. And then he was sprawled into the warm dryness as though he'd just awakened from a nap on the beach.

He opened his eyes and unconsciously looked at his hands to make certain they were still attached. He turned in the loose sand. The gang was spread across the top of the cliff as though they were collectively on the verge of following him. Filthy's hands came together in a clap and a grin ripped his face. But the rest only stared. The Weasel was slack-jawed, his cigarette gone.

You crawled out of the sand and jogged down the track in the opposite direction from which they'd come. He knew where some vines overhung the cliff. It would be a lot faster than going all the way up the road and through the mountain laurels again. He hauled himself up hand over hand, walking his feet up the rock.

The Mazarsko twins came over to meet him and escort him back to the clearing. They chattered in the shorthand they sometimes used, slapping him on the back as they went.

As he entered the clearing, You walked past the outstretched hands, turned, and again ran past them and launched himself off the overhang. This time he kept his eyes open and spread his arms like an eagle's wings. The little spill of sand grew as he approached it. He relaxed as he hit, splaying himself across the friendly sand.

For a long moment no one moved. Several of the gang looked at each other, hoping someone would say something. No one did.

"Hey! What're you kids doin' messin' up that sand?" the foreman yelled from up the road.

You got his feet under him to make a run for it, and headed again for the obliging vines. The gang scattered into the woods as though they'd never been there.

Spurred by the possibility of getting caught by the foreman and getting the shit beat out of him by his father when he found out about it, You clambered up the vines and disappeared into the greenery. He peered from behind a tree and watched the foreman make a half-menacing shake of his fist. "Damned kids!" he said before turning to walk to the office.

You made his way back to the clearing. Cookies were scattered about, and amidst the two empty beer bottles and the one emptying itself slowly as it lay on its side, he found two full bottles. Hank's church key was still on the rock. He popped the cap off a bottle and took a long drink of warm beer. It made him belch.

He sat the bottle down carefully so that it would wait for him, ran down the clearing and again launched himself. As he floated through the lazy, slow air, all connection with the earth evaporated.

*Originally published in Carver Magazine, 1999.*

# Kryptonite in a Bottle

It happened again! In tuning the television to "Yan Can Cook" on the local **PBS** station yesterday afternoon in hopes of learning how to whip up Lemon Chicken for Two, I inadvertently passed through The Talk Show Zone. There was a plump young woman I'd never heard of talking up something I had heard of before: how women are nurturing and sensitive and how men are aggressive, violent beasts—especially the King Beasts, middle-aged white men with jobs.

The bastards are an affront to all that is good and promising as well as to all that has historically been good but unfulfilled. The pricks are the cause of all evil. They're so damned aggressive, so damned violent. And they dress so boringly, like automatons.

Of course, then the obvious occurred to me. When was the last time you saw a middle-aged guy in a three-piece suit and a rep tie in a police line-up for suspicion of murder, rape, assault with a deadly weapon, a drive-by shooting, or for robbing some little old lady as she made a withdrawal from an ATM?

I caught a wave of revulsion and channel-surfed away from the much Xeroxed bitching show, droplets of stress sweat turning my armpits into fragrant cesspools of anxiousness, my shaking hand grasping desperately for the lifeline of the calming though excitable Yan. When I finally located him within the TV stew, the show had already begun. He was, with great gusto and relish, rendering a meticulously plucked plump-as-a-Sophie-Tucker-breast capon.

It was just too much. I now recast my culinary hero as "Yan the Knife-Wielding, All-Male Butcher Man." The bejeweled matrons in the studio audience slouched forward, mesmerized—either by perverse fascination with the violence, or abject disgust. I couldn't tell which. I snapped off the television in a primordial shame induced by madman Yan cleavering a well-endowed plastic-surgery-enhanced chicken, changed into my running shoes, and headed out the door to escape the assault of violence and male aggression that apparently permeates both television and our society today.

By the time I'd beaten my broken-down, violence- and aggression-prone, stinking male body along a serial of lonely country roads for forty minutes, I felt better about myself. I'd never in my life struck a female and couldn't recall that I had any pressing plans to do so. And none of my male friends had cultivated much expertise in beating up on women, either. And none of them would be considered—at least by other men—to be geeks or simps.

In fact, in one of those moments of revelation that come in the middle of a run, it occurred to me that maybe some of this men-as-violent-beasts world view had it backwards. I time-scudded a bunch of decades backwards, well past memories of the terminal damage Julia Child regularly visited upon defenseless capons. One can rationalize that in the same way Benny Hill may have harbored some female genes (he looked good in a dress). Julia may have been afflicted with a few rogue male genes occasionally yearning for a nip of chaos, havoc, and mayhem. No, that was too easy. My brand-stinking-new theory made more sense—boys learned violent behavior from girls.

At ten years of age, the guys in my fourth grade class at St. Joe's in the central-eastern Pennsylvania burg of East Mauch Chunk were heavily into relatively nonviolent addictions such as trading baseball cards, smoking rolled-up dried rhododendron leaves, and devouring hyper-violent superhero comic books—the simpleton comic books where most of us were on the side of Good, no matter how damned violent Hawkman was forced to become in order to implement the Golden Rule among villains. Inspired by the ideals of superherodom, we went through a phase where we roamed the neighborhood begging old pillow cases and bed sheets that we could turn into Superman or Batman or Green Lantern capes by the artistic application of a pound of Crayola crayons, the capes secured around our necks with an oversized safety pin borrowed from a younger sibling's diapers.

Unfortunately, while we were preparing to save the world from a berserk army of robot monsters from Mars, the she-males in the fourth grade were plotting how they could haul some of our fine young asses away from those burning superhero directives and into playing spin-the-bottle on a lazy Saturday afternoon while the mother of one of the girls went shopping and the house was as empty as the Batcave during one of The Joker's crime sprees in Gotham City.

Canny far beyond the range of mere mortal men, the girls managed to outsmart us one day by telling us it was Eleanor Finley's birthday, and that there'd be plenty of RC Cola and cake at her party. And, we wouldn't even have to bring presents. A "presentless" birthday party! We wouldn't have to blow our allowances just to buy goofy Eleanor 16-ounce bottles of body lotion from the local Newberry 5 & 10 Cent Store. Just come on by and eat all the sweet junk your young, hardy stomach can hold. It was an inspired ruse.

A half-dozen of us trooped uptown to Eleanor's, several of us sporting our newly completed superhero capes, leaping off every tall wall we could find along the way, outracing speeding delivery trucks. We actually were looking forward to reaching Eleanor's house because she lived in the middle of a block of row houses built on a hill, and her front porch was a good eight or nine feet above a scrawny little lawn—a perfect superhero launch-pad porch, a perfect little landing area yard with already scuffed–up, nearly dead grass that we wouldn't get yelled at for ruining.

When we arrived, we took a few preliminary leaps off Eleanor's front porch onto the lawn, employing the appropriate flying sounds of a human projectile hurtling through the upper atmosphere, our magnificent capes flowing gloriously out behind us. The young ladies sat primly on the front porch swing, whispering among themselves and indulging our antics—for a few minutes.

But after what seemed like no time at all, the talk turned to cake and RC Cola. We'd worked up quite an appetite saving these young ladies from threatening meteorites, evil villains, and mole people, so we were amenable to grubbing down and refueling our depleted energy tanks.

"Where's your mom?" Neil "Batman" Capek asked. Using a pair of artistic scissors, Neil had carefully modified a Mickey Mouse cap with ears into the more sinister bat ears needed to complete his dark ensemble. He'd then pasted some black electrical tape across Mickey's eyes so he looked like a Mafia hit man rendered anonymous in Police Gazette.

"Oh," Eleanor said, "she's at the store. She won't be back for a little while."

Okay, we thought, she's a light-year more liberal than our moms would be, but if it was okay with her, it was okay with us. Eleanor opened the front door to usher us inside, but as the door swung eerily inward on hinges badly in need of a shot of 3-in-1 Oil, every superhero froze in his tracks, as though struck by the deadly and disabling ray of that evil genius, Ice Man.

Squatting in the middle of the scuffed hardwood floor like a pagan god was that symbol of female domination—the empty glass milk bottle. Heretics caught up in the Spanish Inquisition experienced no greater fear. The big-mouthed glass Bear Creek Dairy bottle, which just that morning had held nothing more dangerous than artery-clogging cow's milk, waited malevolently to be spun, waited contentedly to point at someone who would then be forced to submit to a fate worse than the deadly embrace of Doc Scorpion. In something akin to what in future years would be known as a class-action suit, we collectively balked.

I sidled over to the porch railing, my knees unsteady. I needed to be near something which I could grasp as an anchor providing me with super strength against being pulled through the maw of that open front door. I climbed up on the railing and sat on it, facing away from the house. I lurched through the superhero problem-resolution files stored in my fevered brain, wondering frantically what Superman would do in a sticky situation like this.

Eleanor and her friends began to aggressively work on

persuading us to go inside the now-haunted house, to cross the threshold of terror. They went so far as to question our manhood if we refused to acquiesce to their wanton, amorous desires.

I said nothing, my young muscles of steel coiled to make the leap of a lifetime off the porch, perhaps by that method distancing myself a light-year from the dark, looming doorway.

Rosemary Kelley began to talk to me in a voice filled with gentleness and honey, trying to persuade me to turn around and abandon myself to the unspeakable fate they had in store for us. It was a tone of voice I'd never before heard slither from Rosemary's throat. Her father ran a corner bar and was used to communicating in words not easily located in a standard dictionary, and Rosemary adored her father. Her usual style of dealing with the males in her class was intimidation and threats, some of them physical, a few of which she had followed through on.

She fidgeted and moved her hands nervously behind me as though she'd stuck her hands up to her elbows in itching powder. But true to the unwritten precepts of superherodom, I held firm against her entreaties and hand-wringing. "No way!" I resolutely told Rosemary, and putting action to my manly words, I jumped up and out, away from the coven of vicious females. It was indeed a mighty leap, the steely tendons and muscles in my legs fulfilling their tremendous potential to launch me heavenward.

But my leap was abruptly interrupted, as though by a huge hand that grabbed me from behind and spun me dangerously close to the side of the porch, choking me as I fell—and fell.

I stopped with a jolt, still three feet from the ground.

There was a terrible moment when it felt as though huge hands were clasped around my neck choking the life out of me. My throat was constricted and my tongue came out of my mouth of its own volition, like when a steer's been clobbered on the head with a sledgehammer, and a terrible sound, like a T. Rex attempting to vomit, tried vainly to force itself up and out of my clenched throat.

I was hanging helplessly from the end of my own supercape, the other end of which Rosemary's restless hands had tied around the porch railing while I had naively kept my back turned to her connivery. I was obviously going to die, strangled by my own cape! The utter embarrassment! The shame! I heard the voices of my panicked fellow superheroes as they jumped off the porch to come to the aid of their stricken comrade while the peel of evil female laughter slashed at us like the busy scythes of Dr. Doom.

There was suddenly the sound of a mighty, earth-rending, drawn-out rip, and I knew that the Superman cape I'd spent two long weekends crayoning was no more. At the same moment, the safety pin with the pink plastic catch that I'd borrowed from my little sister's diaper came apart, and my scruffy, doomed body dropped the remaining three feet to the equally scruffy ground.

I floundered for a moment like a beached trout. On my hands and knees, from somewhere inside the pathetic little heap I'd become, I gasped desperately for air.

I turned slowly to see my magnificent cape dangling in tatters from the porch railing as my fellow superheroes gently helped me to my unsteady legs. I coughed and gasped while over my own ugly gurgles and guttural sounds I heard the girls up on the porch laughing—laughing!

My face was nearly as red from embarrassment as it was blue from nearly strangling, but with a heroic effort, I gasped out, "I hate you! I'll get you for this!"

I turned with a speed that would have impressed even The Flash, ran across town to where the forest began in earnest, and found a place where I could safely lick my wounds away from the critical gaze of those (or any other) aggressive girls. I was thoroughly broken and disillusioned. Not even Superman was safe against their mysterious, aggressive, violent, debilitating powers.

Neil "Batman" Capek, one of my rescuing fellow superheroes that day, would eight years later marry the diabolical Rosemary Kelley, perhaps figuring that someday her father would make him a partner in his bar. In spite of all the money Neil spent in the place over the years in an attempt to come to grips with life with Rosemary, Mr. Kelley never did make Neil a partner.

Rosemary bore five children (all girls), and was seen more than once vigorously (and some have said, gleefully) striking Neil about the head and shoulders with a broom. It's enough to make a superhero's heart break. Or perhaps serve as fodder for a talk show.

Nah. They'd never buy it.

# Frogs

The embossed envelope from Kenny Snyder sat on my desk like a sheathed hari-kari knife. Legal-sized, it was three-colored on very lush paper—and opaque, so that, even held up to an X-ray, it would reveal nothing. But without slitting it open, I knew the envelope contained temptation. It was postmarked the day before Kenny's death. It very likely contained the ultimate temptation—to follow him, even there.

The press, which Kenny had so skillfully manipulated, managed to get in the last pun: Frog Man Croaks! That was from the Sacramento Gazette. Two decades ago, when Kenny and his champion frogs threatened to boycott the Jumping Frog Jubilee at Angels Camp in the California Mother Lode over the potential inclusion of huge toothed African frogs, the same paper had screamed, Frog Man Puts Bite On Fanged African Croakers.

Consistently reclusive or extravagantly apparent, whichever suited his objectives at the time, Kenny Snyder was the Michael Jackson of exotic foods. After threatening to boycott the Jubilee that year, he'd arrived in his motorized wheelchair with yet another brace of carefully pedigreed frogs half the size of the African monsters. Kenny's frogs were capable of jumping 50 percent farther than the behemoths. He was quite the breeder. He was quite the showman. He was quite something.

I should mention here, as part of my disclosure policy, that Kenny Snyder and I are related—distantly. Like fourth cousins or something on my mother's and his father's side. But in spite of those ties, we're very different people. Oh yes.

Although we both grew up in East Mauch Chunk, Pennsylvania (a town of about 3,000 people when we were kids back in the '50s), we didn't know each other well when we were little. I lived at one end of town, down near the river and the railroad tracks, and Kenny lived at the other end of town, out in what we used to call "the country," which was any place more than two miles inland from the river's bank. We were further separated because he went to Catholic school and I didn't.

We came together as eight-year-olds when our parents sent us to a summer camp just outside of town for two weeks and we ended up occupying surplus army cots next to each other in a smelly green surplus army tent—where, thankfully, the sides rolled up to let in some air.

Camp was every guy's dream. The woods were infested with flying squirrels so agile that in two weeks, faced with an army of eight-, nine-, and ten-year-old supercharged boys, not one was caught. There were three or four springs in the woods above the camp that emptied into green, deeply shaded pools before the overflow emptied into the cinder-block swimming pool. In the green pools, dappled by sun slicing through the overhanging trees, frogs propagated and crooned their husky songs and, unlike the squirrels, could be caught—and studied and played with and traded back and forth and made to compete with each other in contests of strength and agility.

During our first full day at camp, after spending a sweaty hour clearing rocks from what would eventually become our baseball field (one of the older guys claimed the five-acre parcel "grew" rocks each year like some fields grew corn), Kenny led me to one of the shaded pools to collect frogs. For all our hyperkinetic ways, Kenny and I were eternally patient at the pools. We came back with five handsome frogs in less than an hour, put them in a cardboard box under Kenny's bed, and late that afternoon jumped them against frogs owned and trained by the Kuhn brothers.

It was apparent from the start that one of our frogs was something special. He boasted an extra helping of bright yellow near the shoulders and when spooked by a loud noise, his jumps were prodigious. We therefore called him "Mr. Spooks," and for ten days he was invincible. We turned down enormous offers for Mr. Spooks. One evening we were actually forced to use baseball bats to turn back a trio of guys from another tent who'd snuck through the woods in an attempt to kidnap the lusted-after Spooks.

Even more popular than frog-jumping contests, though, were games of leaveo, which were played every other night just before dark, and in which Kenny and I found our forte.

The rules of leaveo are simple. The entire camp is divided into two teams. A goal/prison is established—in this case, the open, front end of the porch of the main building. The home team guards the goal/prison while sending out hunting parties. The game begins when the home team goes into a huddle, covers its collective eyes, and counts to one hundred. The opposing team scatters to the winds to evade the hunting parties sent out to capture them.

The hunting parties scour the woods, flush out one of

the renegades, pursue him and, upon catching him, grab him long enough to yell, "Leaveo! Leaveo! Leaveo!" At that point, the renegade becomes a prisoner and is led back to the goal/prison. The prisoners, however, can be released to disappear again into the woods if one of the still free renegades can make his way past the prison guards and into the prison, where he must touch one of the prisoners and yell, "Leaveo! Leaveo! Leaveo!"

Each of the games lasts until all renegades are imprisoned or until the home team gives up after an hour or two of futile attempts to round up the last of them.

In the seven games of leaveo contested during the two weeks at summer camp, Kenny and I were never caught once. We had the rare capacity for boys of that age to burrow down under a pile of dead leaves and vanish, keeping so still that a hunting party could walk right past us, even walk on one of our hands, and all they'd think they'd encountered was a dry branch. We were also as agile as monkeys, and several times climbed trees so high that nobody even thought to tilt their heads back that far to search the branches. Hiding in a tree is dangerous, though, because besides the fact that you have nowhere to run to if you're spotted, the other team was not above shaking would-be monkeys down out of a tree.

Not that we always played it safe, though. As soon as half of our team of renegades were captured, we'd begin to play loose in order to free our teammates, coming out of our perfect camouflages for well-executed rescue missions. Typically, one of us would come running out of the woods and head downhill toward the porch, yelling like a maniac, picking up tremendous speed. By the time he came near the porch, he would veer off to one side, drawing the guards away while the other guy would sneak along the side of the building and free a handful of prisoners.

One night near the end of the second week, Kenny pulled what I still think of as the greatest coup of the summer. When the opposing team hid their eyes to count to one hundred and the rest of us took off in a flurry with a chorus of whoops and shrieks, Kenny dropped to his knees and from there rolled under the porch. He calmly lay under the porch until the propitious moment, then rolled out, touched some friendly hands, yelled, "Leaveo! Leaveo! Leaveo!" and was gone into the night.

In fact, that entire day was more than memorable in both happy and sad ways.

We'd been living in the woods long enough at that point to progress to our wild-Indian stage. Bit by bit, we had scrubbed off the veneer of civilization. Earlier that day, I'd managed to beat the reigning ten-year-old in Mumblety peg. He'd become so irate at losing that he'd tried to stick his knife into my foot. When he finally did just that, I stood there, my legs stretched out to nearly a split, and didn't utter a sound. Several of the other guys yelled bloody murder, though, and pretty soon a counselor was on hand, removing the offending knife from my foot, asking if I'd had a tetanus shot, and reaming out the ten-year-old real good. He got put on Aunt Gussy duty, which meant that at the end of the week he'd get to go down "The Hole" and bucket out the outhouse.

The sight of blood inspired Kenny to suggest that we become blood brothers by cutting our thumbs and comingling our blood like the Indians did. He'd suggested the same thing a week earlier and I'd resisted, but now, seeing my own blood seeping through the canvas of my sneaker, I thought, "What the heck?" Kids must have buckets of antibodies onboard, because neither cut ever festered even when, a half-hour later, we used our bloodied hands to fish out poor Mr. Spooks who, after gallantly and uncompromisingly representing our tent in the frog jumps, had died sometime during that hot day.

After the excitement of our leaveo victory died down, and well after curfew, we crept from the tent (Kenny in the lead), found a lonesome spot in the woods, built a little fire, and roasted Mr. Spooks like a pig on a spit. Kenny theorized that if we ate Mr. Spooks, we would be imbued with some of his jumping and swimming abilities, just as taking Communion at church on Sunday, you are imbued with the body and blood and spirit of Christ. The things they teach kids at Catholic schools . . . .

Mr. Spooks's skin blistered and burned pretty good and we hadn't removed his insides, which boiled into a real mess and turned my stomach—but not Kenny's. He did manage to get me to eat one of Mr. Spooks' legs while he ate the other and just about everything else, even the little heart. I'm usually finicky about eating unusual things. But Kenny already knew at age eight that they did that kind of thing in France and actually considered it cool.

I don't remember much about what that leg tasted like, but we didn't get sick or die, and over the last few weeks of summer, we attributed our increased running, jumping, and swimming abilities not to our rapidly developing young bodies, but to the spirit of Mr. Spooks living within us. Kenny's developing physical abilities seemed to always be one step ahead of my own, which he attributed to his disproportionate feasting on Mr. Spooks.

By the time the summer did that weird thing summers used to do toward the end, where the lazy, sometimes boring days vanish to be replaced by rapid days of half the hours they had in July, Kenny and I were more than best friends and blood brothers. We had progressed to the point where we were going to be best buddies forever. We had it all figured out.

The next summer, we were going to spend the whole summer together. But it didn't work out that way. Little did we know that the amazing spirit of Mr. Spooks was already working away inside us, eating away our souls with a moral cancer from which we'd never be cured.

At Christmas, we both managed to cajole our parents into buying us bicycles. Now completely mobile, we spent the first half of that summer extending our realm of influence. We included daily excursions to the summer camp out beyond town to monitor progress on draining and cleaning the pool, because when that was done, the two weeks of heaven would begin. It took a good four days for the spring water to refill the pool, and a day or two after it had filled, camp began.

By that measuring stick, it would have been two days after the pool was cleaned that we headed, from opposite ends of town, to the camp. It was a bright summer day, with just a bit of a breeze. Both of us arrived in less than optimal moods, I recall. I don't remember what had gotten under Kenny's butt, but my less than cheerful attitude revolved around not having spread the coal furnace ashes the way my Dad wanted them spread after I'd emptied them down at the end of the backyard. I don't know, I must have been daydreaming, or looking forward to getting out of there or something, but I got my britches warmed and was told I'd have to be home an hour earlier than usual, as punishment. Ah, the good old days of corporal and infallible punishment.

Kenny had arrived at the campground before me, and had parked his bike up in the woods—so that if somebody came by they wouldn't know we were there. He'd already begun scouting around for good leaveo hiding places in the woods near the spring-fed pools, since it was a good place to hide and never be found—because, after dark, very few kids would venture anywhere near the pools. They were too much like the dreaded Loxahatchee Swamp in Florida.

When I arrived, ruminating about my unjust punishment, I put my bike with his and began looking for him. From the place I was on the hillside, I could see that the swimming pool was only about half-filled. The entire shallow half was dry, except for where the water was coming in. I didn't want to yell for Kenny, because to do so might alert someone who lived near the campground that there were prowlers, so I tracked him down.

He was kneeling beside one of the shadowed pools, stalking a bullfrog. I crept up silently, watching him work. The pool was like a holy place, quiet and cool, water bugs skimming the flat surface. He was a real master at the quick grab, sort of like a python striking out at its supper. Once in position, he seldom missed his target. This time, he grabbed a medium-sized croaker and quickly held it up to the light to admire it, holding it by the thighs so it couldn't squirm away.

I applauded briefly. Kenny looked up, startled, then saw

me and waved his free hand and held up his catch. "They're everywhere this year," he said simply, looking to both sides of the pond, where an occasional splash indicated that another croaker had gone after a bug or had jumped into the water to cool off.

He brought the frog over, petting its head. It was a good healthy one—that was for sure. Its dark green upper body was shiny and slick, its underside the color of chicken skin. Its prominent eyes looked around dumbly, and it breathed quickly, its body expanding and contracting.

"What'll we do with it?" I asked.

"Let's put him in the swimming pool," Kenny said. "We'll let him jump around the low part."

"Okay," I said. "But wait a minute till I get one, too."

The frogs were so plentiful that it literally only took a minute, and I had a croaker of about the same size. We walked with them down to the low part of the pool, which was still dry, and put them in. Both frogs looked around as though totally confused, then one of them made a small, tentative leap. The other sat, not certain what to do. Kenny watched them almost dreamily, as though his mind was somewhere else. I jumped behind the frog that just sat there, and when I came down with a crack of my high-top sneakers on the hard pool bottom, the frog took a good-sized hop.

"Let's get as many as we can and fill the pool," Kenny said. "When somebody comes by and sees them, they'll think we've been invaded."

We spent the next hour or two running back and forth between the shallow, dry end of the pool and the spring-fed pools, catching hapless frogs and rapidly transporting them down to the pool. We must have had forty or fifty frogs sitting in the shallow part looking around, wondering who had called the frog convention. They did not seem like a particularly active group.

In retrospect, I can see that what had been happening was that the heat of the nearly high-noon sun was baking the frogs by heating them from above and frying the cinder-blocks under them. They had become torpid and sluggish and were too stupid or too tired to make the thirty-foot trip to the water in the deeper end of the pool.

For some reason, this angered Kenny, as though one of his close relatives had been found to be retarded and it somehow reflected on him.

He knelt down and tried to egg one of the frogs on by tweaking its ass. The frog just sat there. He tried it with another. Nothing. The sun was beating down mercilessly and the frogs were drying out and going rapidly toward that big hibernation. Nothing seemed to motivate them. We were surrounded by dozens of nearly dead frogs.

Kenny picked one of them up. "Jesus," he said, "their slime is even different."

I bent down and ran my finger along the back of one of the listless frogs. The slime was different. It had become less viscous, more sticky.

"I'd better save this guy's life," Kenny said, and in a smooth motion he underhandedly threw the frog into the air the way you'd lob a softball to a girl. The frog sailed through the air toward the water in the deep end of the pool. But Kenny had miscalculated. Instead of plopping into the saving water, the frog fell onto hard cinder-block pool bottom and splatted. It didn't explode or anything, like in a cartoon, but we could both tell by the sound that the fog was a goner.

I ran up to the frog. An experienced enough ballplayer

that he knew the pitch was inadequate to reach the plate, Kenny had frozen on the spot the second the frog left his hand. Maybe it was the tackiness of the slime on the frog's body that caused it to stick a bit too much to Kenny's palm—and fall short. Kenny walked up slowly.

I was already kneeling next to the frog, examining it. It looked like a deflated beanbag. And its guts were just barely visible, trying to get out the half-opened mouth. The frog was very much dead.

"Jesus," Kenny said. "What a mess."

"What're we gonna do?" I asked.

"I ain't touching no dead frog," Kenny said, suddenly fastidious. He'd touched lots of dead frogs before. Hell, he'd even eaten most of Mr. Spooks, and that after he'd been dead who knows how many hours?

His sudden aloofness to the situation he'd caused riled me. Stoked by the embers of resentment at the treatment I'd received from my father earlier in the day, I ran back to the shallow end of the pool, picked up a sluggish frog, and threw it with all my strength at Kenny. Still regarding the dead frog at his feet, Kenny didn't bother to see it coming. It hit him square in the back, made a softer splat sound than the frog that had hit the bottom of the pool, and dropped at his feet, either dead or very close to it.

For a second Kenny was stunned—but only for a second. In that second, a lot of stuff rushed back and forth in his head—a lot of stuff modified by his Catholic education. And I assume the Catholic education lost, because he picked up the frog I'd thrown at him, and threw it at me. I saw it coming and jumped out of the way. The dead frog sailed past and skidded along the dry pool bottom.

I retaliated with another frog bomb, and Kenny fought

back in kind. At some point during the mindless exchange, however, our cruelty turned against the frogs not as a secondary agenda item, but directly. Kenny had just sidestepped another of my fastballs. He bent down, picked up a nearly dead, sun-bleached frog, and threw it with all his might at the hard pool bottom right in front of his feet. There was so much force, so much anger behind the throw, that this time the frog did sort of explode.

Seeing what he'd done, Kenny took an attitude of "They can only fry me once" and began walking around the pool, pitching frogs down to their deaths. By the sixth or seventh frog, the same death lust filled me, and I began running around, looking for unexploded frogs to detonate. I don't know how long the whole thing took. It seems it was at once both endless and immediate.

But suddenly, with no more breathing frogs left in the arena, we both stood there, at opposite sides of the shallow end of the pool, looking at each other from under lowered brows, panting as though we'd just run a race. The pool was a mess, like the shank end of a nasty war.

Neither of us said a word.

I shuffled off to my bicycle, cached up in the woods, walking head-down, as I would have if I were the only one for miles. I wiped my guilty, slimy hands on my jeans and got on the bike and rode home, ruminating all the way. I never looked back.

I heard through my mother, who persisted in trying to mend whatever had torn us apart, that Kenny had taken to his bed with some terrible summertime flu, and that he stayed in bed for three days, sweating, shivering, and vomiting up some foul green gruel. Then, as quickly as it came, his sickness passed.

The next week, when camp started, Kenny didn't show up. There was a big stink about the dead frogs in the pool. They'd had to drain the pool again and refill it with bitter cold water so only the terminally brave got the opportunity to swim toward the end of that summer's camp session.

I didn't see Kenny again for years, and then only when he was driven through town in his parents' car—and later, driving his own car. In retrospect, I realized that I didn't make as much of an attempt as I might have to reestablish contact, because the thing that was preventing that from happening wasn't something so much between Kenny and me as it was something that each of us was fighting within ourselves.

I do know that Kenny's mother wanted him to enter the seminary after high school, but he persisted in his own notions. He went to East Stroudsburg State College to become a gym teacher, while I went to Espy State, a good hour's drive along Interstate 80 between us. Once, during that time, he wrote me a letter, but I didn't even open it. I had by then rewritten history: Kenny Snyder had led me into shaming myself in the dry end of the camp swimming pool and I didn't ever want to give him another chance to do that again.

This was the mid-1960s. Rather than wait to be drafted after graduation from college, Kenny joined the Navy and became a SEAL. It came as no surprise to me to learn that they had evolved from the World War II frogmen and that they specialize in amphibious assaults, going in early and clearing the beaches of obstacles, or doing sensitive work, like creeping up rivers and skulking onto land to cause mischief. From what I heard over the years, Kenny's childhood spent in the woods and his mastery of leaveo stood him in good stead in Vietnam. Rumor has it that he was also very good with piano wire.

He moved to California after he left the military. Out there he made a name for himself as a swimmer. He tried out for the 1972 Olympic team but after qualifying was put off the team for failing some sort of blood test. We all suspected drugs. On later reflection, I wasn't so sure.

In 1976, he tried out for the Olympic team again, this time in two events, what were then called the broad jump and the hop, skip, and jump, which are now called the long jump and the triple jump. Again, he made the team, only to be disqualified later and booted off for some technical reason.

While periodically under the influence of good pot or too much red wine, I conjured up a theory—to explain his dismissals—that had to do with some type of genetic irregularities in my old friend, perhaps precipitated by having ingested too much of Mr. Spooks.

For a while Kenny vanished from the scene, but not long after moving to California myself in 1978, I read about him in conjunction with the annual Frog Jumping Jubilee. His frogs had won two years in a row and his frog-leg company, Copper Amphibians—outside Copperopolis—was apparently the most famous frog ranch in the world. He exported gourmet frog legs to France, as well as to French restaurants in Montreal, New York, Baton Rouge, and New Orleans. He raised one very special species of frog whose legs he exported to France under the appellation Le Grand Cru des

Grenoilles—ils ont de la cuisse! They're big, they're juicy, they have a delicate hint of gaminess, and the French go crazy for them.

Somehow he found out that I'd moved to Northern California. Twice he left messages on my answering machine, seemingly good-natured messages that were tinged with a slightly sarcastic edge I knew only too well. He wanted me to become a partner in his company. The thought of all those severed frog legs sickened me.

By that point in my life, I felt not apathy about reestablishing contact with cousin Kenny, but actual fear that he might somehow reopen doors within me that I'd long since locked.

It was excruciating to learn, by way of a small news item, several years later that he'd lost both legs to cancer, but I still couldn't bring myself to call him. Perhaps by building it up over the years, I'd convinced myself that to give in to Kenny was to abandon my very soul.

I consoled myself the next year by closely following the controversy surrounding the entry of the huge African frogs. Kenny had gradually gotten himself more and more into a folksy mode, joined E Clampus Vitus, the riotous historical fraternity descendant from the gold-seeking 49ers, and wore their signal red shirt with black pants, black hat, and black vest whenever appearing in public. You may remember seeing him on network television. His quote was on all the nightly news shows and in all the papers, and they used it even though it was longer than the average sound bite: "If Mark Twain had wanted these African monsters in this here contest" (See how folksy he'd learned to talk? He's from central-eastern Pennsylvania, for God's sake.) "he'd a had Dan'l

Webster be one of 'em, 'cause you know how Twain loved an exaggeration, en he'd a weighted that frog down with cannonballs 'stead a buckshot."

It came out after all the fireworks that Kenny'd had a half-dozen of the African frogs in his collection for years, but felt frogs with teeth would go against the spirit of the whole Jubilee, which is why he never entered any of his own monsters.

Then, a few years ago, on the way back from a skiing trip to Bear Valley, up about an hour above Angels Camp, I stopped at the Murphys Hotel to have some of their famed fried chicken. The couple at the next table was talking about Kenny. He'd apparently just bought some of their property that abutted his own, planning to further expand the frog ranch.

I eavesdropped on them much the same way I'd listened to the conversations of leaveo hunting parties at camp when they were looking for me and I was under a pile of leaves two steps off the path they were on. This rancher was right proud to sell some of his land to Kenny. Seems they found a mutual liking for disliking the French. This old rancher fought in World War II, his father in World War I. Both were of the opinion that for all their annoying pride and bravado, when it had come down to brass tacks, the French (he referred to them, naturally, as "the frogs"), faced with a real enemy in Germany, had rolled over and spread their legs. Kenny Snyder continued the scenario to the Vietnam War, which Kenny claimed we'd gotten into because we'd been dumb enough to give Vietnam back to the French after the Second World War to salve their outrageous egos, and then when they'd allowed things to go down the shitter, they'd hightailed and run, leaving us holding the shitty end of the shovel.

"Guy's gettin' back at 'em by sellin' 'em overpriced frog legs," the rancher said, "an' makin' a fortune off them Frenchies' pride in bein' sophisticated 'nough ta eat that shit." The rancher's wife never said a word during the whole meal. "God, I love ta see somebody git the upper hand on them unprincipled bastards!" the rancher said.

I skipped dessert and left.

On the drive through Copperopolis, I took a bit of a detour to go past Kenny's place. You can't see much from the road, because the big wrought-iron gate keeps the curious from driving up the long, winding road to the house, and I suppose the ponds and such are down in the valley behind the house. But out front, next to the gate, is a very fancy sign bearing the very modern, very contemporary logo of Kenny's company, Copper Amphibians. Within a light green circle below the name is a copper-colored frog leaping from a dark green lily pad.

Under the fancy, professional sign, though, someone— perhaps Kenny himself—had painted another sign in Old Western style: Our Frogs Is Dyin' Fer Yer Sins.

Reading that sign made me wonder just what the hell had gotten into Kenny Snyder. But thinking that thought made me laugh to myself in order to gloss over the cold, clammy feeling I had that I knew exactly what had gotten into Kenny.

I reached again for the fancy envelope on my desk, expecting to feel on it a hint of dried frog sweat. Instead, it was just an expensive envelope with an expensive embossed Copper Amphibians logo, dry and smooth as a final argument. As I'd done before, I carefully held it up to the light but still could not see through it.

And as before, I returned the fancy envelope to its place on my desk, wary of releasing its contents into a life spent hidden under dry leaves.

*Originally published in Carver Magazine, 2002.*

# Big Game

We rode over the Broad Mountain, in the back way to White Haven, and down to the river with the railroad next to it—then along the rutted road, with the rails between the river and us. The gate that 364 days a year kept civilians off railroad property had been opened to accommodate the traditional flood of mostly fair-weather big-game hunters primed for the one-day doe-hunting season. The sheets of ice on top of the puddles in the ruts had been shattered by cars that had arrived early. For a Saturday in October in eastern Pennsylvania, the day was what you'd expect—chrome-bumper cold, and gray as a mothballed battleship.

We drove past a half-dozen cars nudged against the mountainside, not wishing to infringe on their temporary big-game-hunting fiefdom. We passed one car disgorging its Woolrich-encased gaggle of hunters—one of them with Abe Lincoln whiskers common to local Pennsylvania Dutch, luxuriating over coffee in a Thermos top while sitting on the back bumper of a rusted Plymouth.

The dregs of getting up so early on a Saturday morning had been rattled loose. An excitement about arriving at the appointed place filled our car, although it was not strong enough to rouse Big Eddie Duboski, who slept next to me in the back seat like a hibernating bear. Known to his few friends as "Fat Boy," Eddie whistled rather than snored. He smelled of burned bacon and stale cigarettes.

In the front seat, "Rocky," my father, piloted the used '55 Mercury four-door, while Dieter Krug sat next to him. Eddie and Dieter were my father's friends and hunting buddies. I wouldn't realize for some years that Eddie and Dieter were his only two close male friends in the world. To hear him criticize them when they weren't around, though, you'd be sympathetic toward his enemies.

Although my father and Dieter wore thick woolen shirts with collars, the backs of their heads were very recognizable to me. My younger brother Randy and I had spent many a Saturday or Sunday following behind them on hikes in the woods while Fat Boy brought up the rear. Both my father and Dieter went to the same barber, so the late-1950s adult trim along the back of the head was identical. The rough skin on the back of Dieter's neck was more wrinkled and more pitted than my father's, but not by much. My father had a mole peeking through his dark hair on one side in the back. (Moles were part of the family inheritance of being Slovak.) Some stereotyping goes right down to the genetic level.

My father slowed the car and steered it into a little dugout by the side of the road, running slowly through a particularly big puddle whose ice coat had not yet been breached. It tinkled like glass, even over the sound of the car's motor. When the car was turned off and the heater and defroster fan fell silent, the sound of the rushing river intruded. It ran so fast and dark it seemed angry.

"Better wake the Fat Boy," said Dieter.

I reluctantly nudged Mr. Duboski, but nothing happened.

"Wake him up. We're here," my father commanded.

I poked Eddie in the ribs harder and he stirred. I felt reluctant to do too much of anything. I felt like an intruder in the midst of these odd friends, and didn't really want to be there to start with. After resisting my father's hectoring to go deer hunting with him and his friends for years, I'd broken under my mother's insistence that I do it. "Just for this once," she'd said, "then if you don't like it, at least you'll have tried it, and we can have some peace and quiet around here."

My father had a deep and angry need to have both of his boys become carbon copies of him and saw the fact that neither of us was so inclined as a personal affront. Perhaps if he'd been less insistent about it and showed a bit of interest in what we enjoyed, there'd have been some compromise.

Both Randy and I deeply enjoyed the woods, perhaps more genuinely and naturally than our father did, but we didn't enjoy nature on his narrow terms. We'd hiked frequently with him and his friends, taking extravagant pleasure—on a particularly cold day—in manfully sipping coffee from tin cups poured from a pot they'd buried in a secret place far from civilization. The pot was brought to boiling over a small crackling fire, which, in that boyhood phase where all boys are pyromaniacs, we'd always offer to build, only to be reprimanded for doing it not so much wrong as too eagerly for it to be militarily precise. Dieter, a lifelong bachelor, would tell us we were building it just fine and he'd wink at us as he sipped his coffee.

We were never offered coffee at home and never liked it anywhere else but in the woods. Randy and I tried to make our own coffee on our own hikes but it never came out as good.

The caked powdered milk we'd chip from a recycled Ovaltine jar took its time blending and softening the too-strong coffee. At home our father drank coffee through which you could read the classified ads in a newspaper; on the chilly hikes, the darker and stronger the coffee the better. It was Chase & Sanborn tossed into the battered pot by the handful.

In order to force my hand at becoming an outdoorsman of his pedigree—a manly man who belonged to the National Rifle Association and religiously read American Rifleman and reloaded his own ammo and saved discarded "brass" whenever he found it even if it wasn't .270 casings for his rifle—my dad had "built" me a rifle, a .30-06. He'd ordered a surplus military Remington rifle from an ad in the back of American Rifleman. The thing arrived in two pieces in a long box that hadn't been disturbed for decades. Inside was a long stock that weighed lots more than a handful of 42-ounce Ted Williams "Black Beauty" baseball bats, and the barrel and workings, slathered with enough grease to lube a Mack truck, were wrapped up in a light brown sort-of wax paper.

He discarded the heavy dark stock and carved one of his own that, unlike the original, stopped way short of the muzzle; the new stock was of a light-colored wood. He bought a special woodworking tool to etch in crosshatching that provided a better grip.

After laboring for hours to remove all the grease that protected the barrel and the workings, he came as close to divorce as ever in his life when he ordered a trough-like pan about six inches tall that extended over two burners of my mother's gas stove into which he lowered the barrel and then poured in a noxious "bluing" liquid that when heated would cover the barrel with a protective shield against corrosion. The chemical stench filled the kitchen for weeks.

He installed a modern set of open sights, assembled everything, and hauled me to the top of the Broad Mountain so we could sight in the "new" gun. I was expected to be thrilled by having my own weapon. But I saw it as one more maneuver to imprint me as a carbon copy.

He was at once both thrilled and bitter when I easily outshot him with the new gun. (My mother and I were both better shots than he was. It was probably good that he'd spent World War II stationed in Panama training infantry troops on their way to the front on how to avoid getting syphilis rather than leading them into battle.)

We tumbled out of the Merc into the cruel damp autumn. The inside of the car suddenly felt as though it had been a damp tropical swamp.

The trunk bristled with armament, a modern survivalist's wet dream. I carefully retrieved my .30-06 and gently leaned it against the side of the car while I buttoned up my flannel shirt and backed into my Woolrich coat. I buttoned it down as though I were a deep-sea diver. I pulled the wool hat down farther over my ears. My father carefully but professionally removed his .270 and leaned it against the car. Dieter did the same. Eddie was still half-asleep and handled his equipment more nonchalantly, as was his way—the source of one of many bones of contention my father had with Fat Boy.

While the others manfully wrestled with their warm clothes, I looked around at this place I'd never been before. My brother and I had often hiked along the railroad tracks from East Mauch Chunk in this direction, but had never gotten this far. Other than the railroad junction where we'd come in, the site was indistinguishable from most of the real estate along the railroad right of way. Mountains rose steeply from both sides of the rushing river— the contour like the wrinkles on a bloodhound's forehead if they'd been ironed to harsh creases.

It had snowed several times over the previous week, and there were large acreages of snow on those portions of the mountain that received no sunshine. Pointing uphill into the valleys between heaves of the mountain, Dieter and my father were discussing tactics.

The plan was simple. Two of us (my father and I) would hike up one of the valleys while Dieter and Eddie would hike up a parallel one several valleys over. My father and I would reach a ridgeline atop the swell between two valleys and plant ourselves on either side of the ridgeline, each with an unobstructed view of his respective valley. Dieter and Eddie would hike up their valley, reach the top, cut across until they were above our position, then drive the deer (if there were any) down the valleys we were covering. Once the deer entered our fire zone, we would shoot our own deer and then, if possible, a deer for each of the drivers.

I slung my rifle over my shoulder and followed my father up the valley to the right of the nose of our car. Dieter and Eddie walked downriver a bit, then turned up another valley. Eddie, already falling behind, waddled along slowly, like a bear with arthritis.

The climb my father and I made was nothing very ambitious. If it were summer and we weren't burdened with layers of clothes and the rifles, my brother and I could have run up the valley with little effort. We often did just that on Bear Mountain—the mountain behind our house back in town. But today my father and I plodded along, saying nothing. Our job was simple—set up an ambush for the deer.

As far as I was concerned, the less talk the better. I'd stuttered badly since age five, when I'd awakened under ether while having my tonsils removed. My handicap had been one more bitter disappointment for my father; his first-born spawn was increasingly a trial. His reaction to my stuttering had been predictable. He blamed me for it and insisted I did it to gain attention, the last thing in the world a stutterer lusts after—better to turn to liquid and drop down the crack between two floorboards.

The heat of exertion neutralized the damp chill coming off the river and the rocks and the sky and the patches of snow. When we reached the ridgeline, we found an open spot uncluttered by obstacles to the panoramic view of our respective valleys. A vertical rock outcropping ran the length of the ridgeline like the dorsal fin of a swordfish. I snuggled into the rocks on my side, my back against the fin and my rifle sitting across my knees, while my father did the same on the other side. I checked and re-checked the rifle to make certain the rear safety was on, nervous about again screwing something up if I didn't do it exactly the way my father would under the same circumstances.

I had a view of the angry river far below, obstructed only at one point by the peak of the ridge. My valley had steep sides and, under the low gray clouds, was monochromatic: dull white patches of snow and shadow-smudged rocks and occasional bare trees. The few pines stood out like alien intruders.

I tried not to think of the cold, which felt like a corpse holding my cheeks in its hands. I scanned the valley below, my mind wandering. There were a half-dozen books waiting for me at home that I'd rather have been reading at that moment. Half of them were science fiction, which was another of my shortcomings. "Get that nonsense out of your head!" my father would scream at me. "Men are never going to go to the moon. Grow up and fill that space between your ears with something practical!" Something practical—like sitting on my ass on a cold rock on the top of a frigid mountain ridge on a perfectly good Saturday morning.

I wished the Pennsylvania Game Commission would schedule the occasional doe-hunting days on a weekday so I'd be in school. That year there was only one doe-hunting day. They regulated the days based on the deer population. Buck season was always two weeks long, but when the doe herds reached the point where they threatened to outstrip the forage and trigger starvation, they added a one- or two-day doe season to thin the herds.

I personally had no problem with hunting deer. In hikes, I'd come upon enough deer that had starved to death to appreciate the concept of thinning the herd. I also had no problem with hunters shooting deer, especially in eastern Pennsylvania. For some families, the deer meat added some of the only protein they got during the autumn when layoffs and strikes at the mills were common and nourishment came from faded surplus yellow-cardboard-boxed, eager-to-clot powdered milk and off-white flour that didn't seem inclined to mix with any liquid known to man. The government gave out the surplus food once a week at the local fire station. It may have originally been meant to feed soldiers in World War II.

It was just that I wasn't particularly interested in hunting deer—or pheasant or rabbits or squirrels—unless we were really hurting for meat. I must have read too many Tarzan books. Shooting deer (big game) with a high-powered rifle—as opposed to shot-gunning small game like rabbits and grouse—didn't seem very sporting unless you were actually starving. Skulking around in the woods stalking game with a Bowie knife between your teeth seemed as though it gave the game an even chance. Bow hunting also seemed a bit more sporting, but my father and his friends looked down on bow-hunters as degenerates, throwbacks.

Although faithful to scanning the mountainside on my side of the valley for any sign of movement, my mind wandered far and wide, in part as a tonic to sitting on a cold rock on a cold day with a cold rifle lying across my cold legs, while cold clouds thickened overhead and threatened to come down to ground level. When my nose ran too much, I wiped it by running the arm of my coat across it. The arm began to look like a herd of snails had stampeded along it. I knew enough not to blow my nose and scare away the deer.

I compulsively reviewed the steps I'd taken to load the rifle, checked that the rear sights were clear and ready. I checked and rechecked the rear safety. My father had a scope on his .270, something that seemed to me excessive. We weren't Eisenhower's boys working as snipers prepared to plug Jerries across the valley.

It occurred to me each time I checked and rechecked my equipment and myself that should some deer be unfortunate enough to wander by and should I perform badly, I'd never again get the chance to do it right. Our father had the habit of giving his sons one chance to do something right; if they did it wrong, that was it. His philosophy wasn't "Try, try again"; it was "Sink or swim."

The realization that I was likely to screw the whole thing up began to work on me. It was how my stuttering worked: The harder I tried to not stutter, the worse it got, a perverse devil cavorting inside my throat and mouth causing havoc. Yet the threat was always present that if it appeared, then I wasn't trying, and I'd be damned as lazy and obstinate.

The implications drained over to this situation. If I did badly today, it would confirm his belief that I was worthless, but if I did well, it would confirm his other belief that I was good at hunting but didn't want to hunt with him just to aggravate him.

I hoped all the deer within the county had left for Florida on vacation. I hoped Dieter and Eddie would become distracted and forget to drive deer toward us, or that all the deer would be on the other side of the mountain.

Then the explosion of the rifle came from behind the dorsal ridge. Rocky must have spotted a deer. Without thinking, I pushed myself off the rock and leapt around the sharp edge of the ridge. It took only a second before I was kneeling next to him, looking down into the valley he'd been surveying, trying to quickly adjust my eyes to the terrain that did not match the valley I'd just spent two hours memorizing.

"Good," he said, meaning that my quick leap to his side of the ridge was a good move. It would remain one of the only times in my life my father would tell me I'd done anything "good."

I surveyed the mountainside across from us, squinted into the gray rocks and the black shadows under trees and the white patches of snow. Barely standing out from the dull spectrums were a half-dozen dun forms standing sideways to us on the mountainside, dumbly looking around.

My father's rifle erupted again, next to my ear. The deer just stood there, frozen.

I threw my rifle up to my shoulder as though it were weightless and stepped through a doorway into a brief/ lengthy world where the focus narrowed down and everything was trapped in amber.

Without conscious thought I flipped the safety off, snuggled my cheek into the stock, sighted through the little rear-sight peephole that seemed enormous once accessed, carefully moved the front sight into the center of the hole as I lined both up on one of the deer. I took a breath, let it out slowly, and squeezed the trigger. The rifle attempted to buck out of my grip but I had it firmly embraced. There was no sensation of the tremendous sound that blasted next to my ear. The smallest of the deer across the valley, which had turned away from me as I fired, fell as though hit between the eyes with a sledgehammer.

I ejected the spent cartridge, snicked in another from the little magazine inside the rifle, and lined up another deer. But before I could shoot it, my father's rifle exploded, his target lurched, looked downhill as though it had dropped something, and fell toward where it was looking. The remaining deer began to move across the mountainside. I rolled my attention to the right, figuring to shoot one of the deer in the lead to head off the others. The sights lined up, I squeezed off the shot, but the deer had stopped. The bullet whzinged off a rock just in front of it.

I cocked the rifle, refocused on the same deer, and

squeezed off another round. The deer jerked up, looked around as though startled, then continued to move off to the right, took four steps, and fell.

As though set free from a trance, the remaining three deer bolted just as my father let loose with a futile shot.

I lowered my rifle. I was a good shot, but not good enough to hit a deer in full flight, and I didn't want to just wing one and let it wander off to die slowly.

I unconsciously reset the safety as I lowered the rifle. The echoes of the last two shots were still bouncing off the surrounding mountains like muffled thunder.

Glancing left at my father, I saw a smile of satisfaction on his face. For a moment he didn't move. Across the valley some blood from the deer my father had shot was seeping into the snow under the animal. The first—smaller—deer I'd shot lay in a little nest formed by a tire-sized rock above it. The other one was down behind a tree.

My father began giving orders. "Pick up your stuff. No sense hiking back up here after we gut the deer. It's downhill from there." He spoke as though his thoughts were being framed in words. He moved with an energy and speed I'd only seen when he regularly came at me or Randy with his belt.

I followed at a slower pace, at two points following his footprints through patches of snow that had warmed enough to become soft again after freezing solid overnight. He hadn't commented on the success of the hunt or on my marksmanship.

When I reached him on the opposite mountainside, he had discarded his equipment, removed his heavy coat, and was gutting his doe. "Take care of yours," he said, pointing farther along the deer trail where mine lay under the rock, having fallen from it.

I leaned over the small deer and ran my hand over it. It was still warm. Its eyes had begun to glaze over. I looked for the fatal bullet wound, but couldn't find it. Bullets make a small hole going in, then begin encountering bones and organs and begin to do more and more damage the more obstacles they encounter, leaving a big exit hole. My father loaded his shells with armor-piercing bullets. They went through cleaner than most and didn't damage as much meat. I had always had the impression from the way he talked about armor-piercing bullets that they'd easily speed through the thickest part of the Hoover Dam if shot at the concrete point-blank. They were guaranteed to leave no molar-cracking shrapnel in the meat.

I probed at the deer, tentative at first, then with more energy as confusion was followed by frustration. How'd it die? I didn't just will it to die. Maybe the sounds of the shooting gave it a heart attack?

I moved the animal to get a better look and then noticed that the bullet that had struck it had done so on its underside, killing it quickly more from shock than typical damage. The bullet had opened a hole in the bottom of it and its internal organs had dropped out, beginning the gutting process for me. The viscera were still warm as I worked with my knife to free them from the body cavity. I was not as squeamish as I'd have been had I had time to think about it. When I reached the back of the deer I encountered a penis. Startled, I reached over its body and felt the top of the head and found two nubs. I'd gone doe hunting and gotten a button buck—a young buck that in deer years was nearly my age. I took a moment longer to examine the deer and, on the second pass, found the entry wound. The bullet had gone directly up the deer's rectum and out the lower chest, effectively gutting it while leaving the hide intact.

As I moved the viscera away from the carcass, attempting to keep as much blood and damage off the hide as possible, my father came over with the heavy rubber bag he'd packed in. The heart and liver and kidneys from his deer were already inside. I felt around in my deer and cut the organs loose and dropped them into his bag just as Dieter arrived.

"It's a buck," I said to Dieter, the liver sliding off my bloody fingers into the bag like a . . . liver. I hated liver, a delicacy my father forced the family to endure as least five or six times a year. Now I'd contributed to our eating liver yet again.

Dieter bent down to check the little buck's head. "Sure enough," he said. He laughed. "Ya got Bambi."

I blinked one long blink and looked at the juvenile deer. He hadn't said it in a vicious way and I wasn't especially sensitive to the whole Bambi mythos. Most forest fires that kill deer are started by nature, after all.

"Yours is over there," my father said. Fat Boy hadn't yet arrived. Dieter looked confused. "He got two of them—" he began, assuming right away that I'd made the shot.

Dieter smiled. "A real big-game hunter," he said. My father handed the bloody rubber bag to Dieter for the deposit of his deer's heart, liver, and kidneys and walked back to his own deer. "How many shots?" Dieter asked before trudging down the trail to work on "his" deer.

I held up three fingers so my father wouldn't hear me. I wasn't sure what was wrong this time, but my father seemed as though he was heating up one of his kettles of rage and I didn't want to take a chance on tipping it by seeming to brag that I'd shot better than he had. Dieter smiled again. "Well, you were pretty smart shooting a small one. He won't be as hard to drag out of here."

Eddie arrived and was assigned to carry the four rifles out while each of us dragged a deer. Back at our starting point, we draped the deer over the car and tied them down securely with rope. At one point, Eddie looped a section of rope through one of the windows and even though it wouldn't have prevented us from closing the door (although the rope would have been flattened) my father fumed. "How the hell do you expect us to get the door closed?"

"We kin close it easy," Eddie said, lighting a cigarette as though he'd just had sex. My father made a point of slamming his door closed before he started up the car.

We drove out of there in various psychological states. Eddie was talkative, telling us step by step how he and Dieter had topped the ridgeline and turned to drive deer before them. Dieter agreed when appropriate. My father drove in silence. I stayed silent, nodding in agreement when Dieter or Eddie seemed to ask for affirmation.

We dropped Dieter and Eddie off at Dieter's and helped them take the deer into Dieter's carport where it was hung up to cool. Dieter brought out a pot and took his liver and heart and all the kidneys out of the plastic bag. It wasn't yet 1:00 p.m.

My father and I drove home in silence.

At home my mother was ebullient, asking questions excitedly that my father and I answered with minimal words or grunts.

We struggled with my father's deer to hang it up in the enclosed porch overnight so the body would cool. My deer, of course, was easier to get up. My mother took the livers and hearts. The hearts would be pickled in vinegar and fresh onions for a week and then would be sliced for use in sandwiches. The livers we'd be forced to eat over the next week, starting that very night.

Without being told, I washed the blood off my hands and from around my fingernails, and then disassembled and cleaned my rifle and put it away.

Later that day, when Randy came home from larking around with his friends, he wanted all the details. I told him little.

Over fried liver and onions that I hardly touched later that night, my father was still moody. My mother, after all those years with Rocky, either didn't get when to let something go or enjoyed sparking trouble. (As the years went by, I reluctantly came to the conclusion that it was the latter.)

"So you did good. I knew you'd like it if you gave it a chance," she said.

"I da-da-da-did-na-na-n't say I la-la-liked it," I said around a dime-sized slab of liver I was masticating like crazy toward being able to swallow and get it out of my mouth. I knew as soon as the words sputtered out of my mouth that I'd crossed the line.

My father stopped swallowing. He didn't chew much, a habit he blamed on being raised in a large family where the "boardinghouse reach" was used—and on being in boot camp fifteen years before where you had to "grab it, eat it, and shit it."

He looked at me with a loathing that would have shocked

me if I hadn't seen it so often before. My mother just kept going on in that way some women do in order to egg a guy on to hit her—to make her stop it. But in this case she was using a surrogate. "But you're going hunting again next year . . . ."

I shook my head very slowly and out of the corner of my eye noticed Randy suddenly slouching in his chair, inch by inch vanishing from the table. "Ya-ya-ya-ya-you wa-wanted me to sha-sha-shoot a deer and a-a-a-a-I da-da-da-da-did."

"Two of 'em!" Randy was good enough to add before his brain caught up with his mouth. He slouched a few more inches, but my father's gaze never turned to Randy. It stayed where it was, a cobra regarding a crippled rodent with due contempt.

I held his cobra gaze and as usual didn't give a hint I was ever going to break. German combined with Slovak stubbornness trumps solo Slovak stubbornness every time. Somewhere outside, a dog barked and a car drove down South Street.

Three eternities and a millennium later he threw his fork on the table and stood up fast enough to nearly topple his chair. He moved to the cellar door, reached around it, and grabbed his heavy coat. "I'll be at Eddie Duboski's," he said, and left, slamming the kitchen door.

For a moment there was silence. We could hear him start up the black Merc, race the engine a moment, then drive off. The silence continued another minute. Randy still slouched in his chair, his brush-cut sticking up like a porcupine.

"Now look what you've done," my mother began.

# Wheels

It's another hangnail kind of winter, with sharp edges and still sharper memories. I wonder how long it will take for my battered memory banks to once again obliterate the feverish memory of Herbert T. "Goober" Schwartz. I can't recall the warped side of my brain dredging up the memory of Goober Schwartz even once during the past decade. Not once. Not even during the occasional nightmare did he come careening around a corner or slithering up through a storm drain.

There was a period, long ago, when my mind used to religiously call him up from the mental junkyard every Fourth of July and every Halloween. But that was back in my freshly post-college, late '60s—back in the unsettled years. After college, with seventy- and eighty-hour workweeks and with moving out of state and all, my memory banks attempted to store too much other information and eventually culled out Schwartz, Herbert T. until I gradually, blissfully thought of him no more.

It's scary, having a culled-out file unexpectedly yanked from the dead-end storage bin of the brain and slapped into the ACTIVE tray like a hundred pounds of freshly-skinned road kill.

When I caught the glimpse of Goober, it didn't click right off that it was him. My younger brother Jack and I were driving down North Street on our way to the Mauch

Chunk Creek Park Watershed to meet his high school cross-country team. Jack's coaching methods include running with his team, even though he's as old as their fathers. Jack feels it's positive reinforcement for the kids, and it's probably good therapy for him, too, now that Irene's left him again. When he was young, Jack was referred to as "King of the Kids" because he spent so much time playing with the younger kids in the neighborhood. They followed him around like a pack of puppies.

I was back in the intimate confines of East Mauch Chunk, Pennsylvania, for a week in late October between business meetings in New York and Philadelphia and was killing off a few weekdays staying with Jack while inflicting myself upon an assortment of old friends. My legs were stiff and tired the way legs become after a bout with the flu or an eighteen-hour flight in coach class. But I knew that mine were sore from simple aging and from spending too much time wedged behind the wheel of a car.

We were noisily roaring down North Street in Jack's rattling MGB, the top down, the late-afternoon air rushing past us with a wind-chill preview of winter. Jack got hooked on British sports cars in college and he's never kicked the habit, in spite of their manifold shortcomings—and shortcomings everywhere else. It was becoming late enough in the year that he'd have to begin the ritual of parking the pile of shit on one of East Mauch Chunk's many hills at night to ensure he could start it in the morning by catching it in gear. Like any British sports car, it balked at temperatures under 45 degrees.

The car's anemic AM radio was turned up full but the wind rushing past our ears, combined with the car's pained mechanical cacophony, was so loud we couldn't even hear the static. As usual, Jack was late and was attempting to make up time that never seemed to wait for him. He revved the piteous motor up to 4500 rpms, shifted to fourth, and we clattered down North Street a good dozen miles per hour over the speed limit. If Mauch Chunk is a circus, North Street is the roller coaster. As we dropped down the sharp hill between Fourth and Third streets, I glanced over to the right, and halfway down the block spotted it.

"What's that?" I yelled at Jack above the wind and the rattling. He followed my gaze as the car chattered over a slight washboard that another car would never have noticed.

The "what" was a lump slumped in a wheelchair that was on its last spokes. The spokes were rusty; the lump was enfolded in several old plaid blankets. The whole ensemble was parked on the small grassy patch between the sidewalk and the curb—between a stunted maple tree making a feeble attempt to show off its sparse fall foliage and an overflowing waist-high green plastic garbage bag.

"What's *what?*" Jack asked, craning his neck.

"The 'what' back there bundled up in old blankets and sitting in an old wheelchair out at curbside as though it's been put out for garbage pickup."

"Must be Goober," Jack said.

"*Goober Schwartz?* He's still alive?" I had no reason to believe Goober Schwartz was dead, but *had* had the decency to assume that time and tide had swept him along into its inevitable vortex, where worthless flotsam disappears when it loiters too long near the drain. Goober, the semi-human flotsam, got a head start on all of us who eventually approach the great suck hole of midlife by taking a swan dive off the Ferris wheel way back there on July 4, 1966.

We used to refer to it in the Mauch Chunks as "The Dive

That Killed Independence Day." To be accurate, though, the time of the dive was never pinpointed. It was more likely an early-morning, July-5th dive than a late-night, July-4th dive. "I subscribe to the July-5th theory, myself," I said out loud.

"What?" Jack asked, downshifting the tired MGB to slow it enough to take the left turn onto Front Street that in turn would lead to River Street that would in turn dump us onto the bridge that would take us over the Lehigh River and across town to Mauch Chunk proper so we could drive up Broadway to get out of town to the watershed and our much-needed workout. In other words, we still had a ways to go.

But in spite of the fact that we were running a little late, I asked Jack to take a swing around the block so I could get a better look at Goober. "I subscribe to the theory that Goober took his dive off the Ferris wheel early morning, July 5th— not late night, July 4th," I explained above the corporation of noises that engulfed us like an institutional-sized clothes dryer half-filled with marbles.

"Yeah, same here," Jack said as he continued to steer us around parked cars sticking partway out onto Front Street. Concentrating on his steering, he half ignored me.

"I can't believe he's still alive," I shouted into Jack's ear.

"Yeah," Jack said. "The guy sure screwed up his family. His mother spends twenty-four hours a day with him, and she might as well be on the planet Mongo for all he knows. And Old Man Schwartz ages two years for every one he lives. He's still trying to pay off the interest from the hospital bills. The rest of the kids were lucky to have a roof kept over their heads long enough for them to get out of high school and get the hell outta here."

"I never liked Goober," I said.

Actually, I can't think of anyone who liked Goober, except for Randy Reinike. And I *should* use Goober's real name when referring to him: Herbert. Herbert T. Schwartz. He didn't get the nickname "Goober" until *after* he took the plunge. And after he took the plunge, everyone tried to like his sorry ass, except for Randy Reinike, who deserted him immediately and for good.

People have this streak where they try to rationalize the existence of someone who's met a calamity, no matter how much of an asshole that person was. At funerals they always work hard to think and say nice things about the deceased, even if the deceased drowned a burlap sack filled with kittens before breakfast every day of his life before beating the kids to a bloody pulp on general principles. Most people do the same thing to assholes who have non-fatal tragedy visited upon them—even if the tragedy is of their own making.

Goober Schwartz is as much a victim of people thinking good after bad as he was of his own inflamed stupidity and meanness. Goober Schwartz holds the dubious distinction of being the first genuinely full-time mean and evil person I ever met in my life. I guess we now refer to them as psychopaths. But having gone through Catholic grade school, I've always thought of him in more simplistic terms: a devil, a creature from hell sent here to remind us every day of the existence of The Master of Darkness.

As I grew older, I went through a stage where I gradually accepted the psychopath handle for such people, but lately I've progressed or perhaps reverted to simply thinking of such people as princes of evil, stone-killers, remorseless

bastards—devils. That allows me to assign the blame somewhere, even if to the theological mythological ether. I don't
go for this psychopath crap. It rejects individual responsibil-
ity, and everyone knows how big I am on accepting respon-
sibility for one's actions. *Shit Doesn't Just Happen, It's A Bowel
Movement of Your Soul.* That's a bumper sticker you don't see
much these days.

Herbert T. Schwartz—and you'd best call him Herbert
and not Herb, or he'd slap you up 'side the head—was three
years older than I was and two years ahead of me at St. Peter's Catholic School. His thyroid kicked in early, so he was
big for his age to start with, which made him doubly fear-
some. He used to regularly beat the shit out of one of us kids
every day at recess.

He'd choose his catch-of-the-day, then work the catch
out of the scattering school of kids and push him over to
the little lawn that bordered the south side of the church.
The lawn was surrounded by a high cement wall on the remaining three sides, and there was a gate behind the church
through which you could access it. That little lawn was the
only green spot on the entire half-block complex of church,
school, rectory, garage, and nuns' convent. Everything else
was concrete or blacktop to keep down maintenance costs
and to create a surface for skinning kids' knees.

Herbert would push his victim through the gate, force
him into the corner formed by the easternmost buttress of
the church, and then begin to methodically slap the living
b'jesus out of him. (As a result of this daily ritual—this
waltzing around on Herbert's part and the ineffectual scuf-
fling on the part of the victim—there was a spot of ground

where no grass grew. The janitor couldn't figure it out. He did everything he could to make grass grow on that spot, even prayed to the saints, but it never took.)

After the thrashing was completed, the victim was informed that he'd best keep his damned trap good and shut or Herbert would kill him on the way home from school and then he'd rape and torture the kid's mother. Nobody ever told on Herbert, not even the Lester twins, whose mother had died when they were born. (She was, therefore, at least theoretically and theologically, beyond the reach of Herbert's evil penis. Unless, of course, she'd inadvertently eaten meat by mistake one Friday, in which case she was burning in Hell's fire, and Herbert T. Schwartz's threat would have been small (baked) potatoes to her way of thinking.)

Herbert was one of those guys in Catholic parochial school who gave rise to the observation that every guy in school is going to grow up to be either a priest or a criminal. Herbert's avowed vocational choice being the latter, he was the recipient of massive amounts of corporal punishment, primarily for his sins of omission, which usually involved his homework, which he brought to class only on days when he remembered to force some other kid to do it for him.

I'll always remember Herbert's knuckles. When it came my turn to get the shit slapped out of me on the patch of ground where no grass grew, I remember his knuckles were always scabby from having been whacked with the ruler— usually a standard-issue ruler with a metal edge (since the plain yardsticks from Marzen's Hardware Store snapped too easily), which is why he always slapped us and never punched us. The level of punishment meted upon his victim was always in direct proportion to the severity and number of whacks he'd taken on the knuckles during the previous week. It illustrated the level of our own saintly/martyr-induced depravity that on the rare days when we were only half-heartedly beaten, we'd wonder after Herbert's mental well-being.

My most vivid memory of Herbert T. Schwartz, however, has nothing to do with school. It has to do with Halloween. It was the Halloween when I was ten years old. Booger Janik and I had been out trick-or-treating for three hours. Booger's parents had bought him the plastic pirate face he'd whined for during the previous week and all evening he'd been sweating like a pig behind it. I was made up as a hobo, which is what I was made up as every Halloween—clothes too big for me and a cork burned over a candle to make black ash that my mother then spit on and smeared all over my cheeks and jaw to resemble a scruffy beard. Years later, in high school, I would theorize that it was spit-laden burnt cork that caused my near-terminal case of zits.

This particular year, Booger and I had literally hit the Halloween jackpot, The Big Spin, tilted the cornucopia of cavity-inducing goodies in our direction. Against our parents' long-standing rules, we'd ventured several blocks beyond our normal after-dark boundaries, and the gamble had paid off BIG! It was the best haul of our lives. One lady, seeing our distress at carrying so much booty, had gone back inside and brought out four Bright's Department Store shopping bags with handles, and now we were headed home, which was five blocks down and two blocks over. Our biggest fear was that the weight of the shopping bags would permanently stretch our arms so that our knuckles would drag on the ground like a gorilla's.

We were talking about giant, radium-scarred gorillas, in fact, not paying much attention to anything, when I looked up and noticed two bigger guys a block away walk into the light thrown by a streetlamp. I stopped in my tracks, recognizing Herbert T. Schwartz's slouching and nearly simian walk. The guy with him I didn't know. It had never occurred to me that Herbert might have friends. Booger took an extra two seconds before he recognized the imminent danger, then he stopped, too.

As one, we crossed the street. Then *they* crossed the street, all the time coming closer. We crossed back onto the other side of the street, where there was more light, hoping it would discourage them, but it didn't. *They* crossed, too.

We stopped dead as they confronted us and, without preamble or small talk, idle threats, or chitchat, Herbert T. Schwartz gave each of us a good whack up beside the head that put stars into the overcast night sky, and while we were stargazing, Herbert and his crony wrestled our shopping bags from us. Herbert's friend then moved in to finish us off, knocking both of us onto the pavement. "Stay there, you sons of bitches," he snarled, bending over us and spraying us with spittle. When he straightened up, he snarled some more, and then they both turned and walked off, happily swinging the bags containing the fruits of our three hours' labor of knocking on doors and singing "A Frog Went A-Courtin'"—all twenty-three stanzas.

Booger and I crawled up off the pavement and Booger muttered, "You dirty pricks!" under his breath. As we turned to walk home, rubbing our sore asses, it began to rain. Booger and I looked at each other in dismay and started to run for home, snot-nosed and crying.

We told our parents that some bigger guys had knocked us down and made off with our treats, but we were careful to feign amnesia about the identity of the perpetrators. My father, the World War II second louie who'd spent the war in Panama training infantry guys in not catching venereal diseases, demanded to know why we hadn't defended ourselves like real men. I guessed he didn't care if Herbert T. Schwartz came in the night and raped and tortured Mom.

But the most painful chapter of the episode came the next morning when Booger and I slouched our depressed way to school in a drizzle that fit our moods. We found our bags of treats ripped apart and the goodies strewn around the alley a block from where we'd been robbed. Herbert T. Schwartz hadn't even wanted the treats to enjoy them; he'd just wanted to make certain Booger and I didn't get that privilege.

There wasn't a thing among the rubble of our labors that hadn't either been broken or turned to slime lumps—being out in the rain all night. We vowed to get Herbert T. Schwartz back someday for what he'd done to us, no matter how long it took, but we never got a chance to fulfill that promise, because Herbert T. Schwartz ultimately robbed us of that as he'd robbed us of so much else we held dear.

It had been tradition in East Mauch Chunk for as long as anyone could remember to have a traveling circus and sideshow come to town for the July 4th holiday. The circus set up in the big field bordering the high school football field—as sorry an excuse for a football field as you'd be likely to find in the civilized world (third-world countries have better playing fields). The circus would arrive a day early and begin assembling itself. The scruffy empty field where we used to spend summer days playing extremely unorganized baseball—with a ball covered with black electrician's tape—was magically transformed into a circus. When we were younger, we'd go up the day the circus arrived to watch the process of unloading and transformation. We'd climb into the trees along the street and sit there for hours sipping RC Cola out of 16-ounce bottles and trading baseball cards back and forth while below us the field—whose every wrinkle and zit we knew so intimately—became a magic place.

Invariably, when the circus workers took a break, several of them would come over to sit under the trees and they'd snarl up at us and give us a hard time. They didn't seem like a very happy bunch of guys and our parents used to warn us to steer clear of the circus people, and when the circus was operating, to never put any of the coins we got in change from the circus booths in our mouths, "because you never know where that money's been"—as though money carried around in great-uncle Sooty's pocket for a week was coated with ambrosia instead of lint and stale goop.

As we grew older, the July-4th circus degenerated. Our sharper, more cynical eyes saw the peeling paint, the shabby posters for the bearded lady, the frayed tuxedo cuffs of the barker, and the bad skin of some of the "hot numbers" who tried to lure you and your money inside a tent for a burlesque show with "more charms of the lovely ladies" on display in a side tent for an extra five bucks. As we grew older, we also found a resentment growing against the guys who traveled with the circus and set it up and manned the booths, especially since it was an annual ritual that several of the more brazen girls in our classes would begin flirting with some of these guys with tattoos and rolls of hard cash stuffed inside dirty bluejean pockets. And stories and smells of towns and cities across the country, that hadn't interested Sally Anne Foster at all in geography class, held her spellbound when elucidated by a circus guy with dirty fingernails and a Texas drawl. Under those circumstances, we'd occasionally felt obliged to defend the dubious honor of our women in little skirmishes which the female caught in the middle always seemed to enjoy in a sort of feline ecstasy that had her pirouetting on her toes like a ballerina.

By July 4, 1966, I was only vaguely interested in the circus at the park. I was between sophomore and junior years at Espy State College, some fifty miles away. I was living at home for the summer while I worked at the Bethlehem Steel's iron foundry. But since the iron foundry was closed for the holiday, the foreman only needed one of us college flunkies to mess around at some janitorial make-work while the place was empty and the fine black sand we used to make molds for iron counterweights for Yale forklifts wasn't flying around like a swarm of sticky May flies. I hadn't picked the short straw that year, so I was off for the day—although not yet in the union long enough to be paid for the holiday.

Since everyone in town seemed to find their way to the circus sometime during the day or night of July 4, it seemed like a good place to go to shoot the bull with some guys I hadn't seen in a year or two and to check out the available action. My brother Jack was at college taking remedial classes in math and English so they'd let him in come September.

Besides, he and I were in one of our periodic mutually despising periods.

I decided to walk to the park after supper. When I arrived, the first guy I saw was Herbert T. Schwartz and his buddy Randy, a kindred spirit with whom Herbert had hooked up once he'd escaped eighth grade in Catholic school and had moved over to public school for the remaining six years of truant-interrupted education—before dropping the pretense halfway through eleventh grade. Randy, it seemed, was public school's answer to Catholic school's Herbert T. Schwartz. Instead of tearing at each others' throats like rabid ferrets when they first met, they saw in each other the best—and worst—of themselves. And, although I didn't know Randy Reinike much at all, Herbert T. was about as narcissistic as they come, so Herbert probably fell in love with Randy's presentation of Herbert on the other side of the two-way ego mirror.

I noted that Herbert T. was still wearing the gravity-defying pompadour he used to comb his hair into when the end-of-day bell rang at St. Pete's. Randy's hairdo was more like a modified surf punk, kind of an off-center crew cut. Both of them were already three sheets to the wind, swigging industrial-strength vodka from a half-gallon jug that sat on the front seat of the convertible against which they were leaning. I assumed by the car's pedigree that it didn't belong to them.

Football in high school, pole-vaulting on the track team in spring, cross country in autumn, and working summers as a Bethlehem Steel laborer had muscled me up pretty good. A dedicated pursuit of the low life hadn't done much to turn

Herbert T. and Randy into impressive physical specimens. Herbert T. was going to flesh around the middle and had skin the color of a toad's belly, and Randy was well-tanned and about as skinny as the pole I used to vault with during spring track. As I walked past them on my way to the circus entrance, they decided on some macho posturing in spite of their physical inability to back it up. Randy said, "Hey, I know you."

I ignored him.

"Hey! I said I know you."

I ignored him some more and walked to the entrance.

The circus seemed to be more rundown than ever. I wondered vaguely if it was the same circus every year, and if so, if they'd ever considered investing in a gallon of paint. I also wondered vaguely if the circus life might not be a good one for Herbert T. and Randy. Herbert T. was chronically underemployed and Randy was working at the Big Cheese hamburger joint in Packerton on the road between Mauch Chunk and Lehighton. Naw, I thought, they might bring the poor circus down a couple more notches toward bankruptcy.

One stroll down the midway was enough to convince me that I wouldn't be making a late night of it. The guys I'd hoped to see weren't anywhere to be found, and almost every female was my mother's age or else not yet out of junior high. Just as darkness came on, as I was seriously thinking of leaving in the wake of a healthy post-supper meal of three chili dogs with onions washed down with two 16-ounce RC Colas, I ran into Larry Lefek, a guy who'd been a year behind me in high school and who'd played guard on the football team. We sat in his beat-up ten-year-old Plymouth for a while and drank some beers he had in a cooler on the back seat while we listened to rock radio from New York City and caught up on life. He was at East Stroudsburg State, majoring in phys ed.

Near ten o'clock, we were about to leave on a cruise to Lehighton looking for some action, when we heard the disturbance over near the Ferris wheel. We decided that whatever it was, it might be the high point of the evening, so we went to check it out.

Sure enough, it was Herbert T. and Randy and two other guys we didn't know causing a ruckus. They were cursing at the guy operating the Ferris wheel. Several other circus guys, recognizing the potential damage to one of their own, had arrived and were managing to hold things in suspension.

Herbert T. was vodka'd to the gills. When he saw us coming over, he must have mistaken us for friends of his who had come to join his side. He could hardly stand, but suddenly he was going to "take on you and a whole army of bastards just like you"—addressing the Ferris-wheel operator over some complaint Larry and I couldn't fathom.

The confrontation was already beginning to fizzle out on its own when two of East Mauch Chunk's finest arrived and gently broke it up. Herbert T. and his bunch wandered off into the darkness, and the circus people, after taking a chiding from the local constabulary, stood around talking for a few more minutes. Ten minutes later, Larry and I left, cruised to Lehighton, and found no more action there than we'd found in East Mauch Chunk. So he brought me back and dropped me off, and I went to bed.

By the time I got home from the day shift at the iron foundry the next evening, the town was frantic.

There were a half-dozen versions of what had happened to poor Herbert T. Schwartz. As I sat down to supper, my mother was erupting with news. "You knew Herbie Schwartz, didn't you?" she asked me. "He went to school with you . . . ?"

"He was two grades ahead, then he was one grade ahead, then he wasn't ahead anymore," I said, feeling sort of nauseous eating with the same mouth that was talking about Herbert T. Schwartz. I was so uninterested in the topic of Herbert T. Schwartz that I didn't even bother to correct my mother by reminding her that his name was *Herbert T. Schwartz* and you'd best not forget it if you didn't want to get raped and tortured. "He was a scumbag back in grade school, and he got lazier as he got older," I said.

The look on my mother's face quickly spelled shock and dismay and "What in the world kind of monster did I raise here?" She was just as quick to inform me that you didn't talk badly about the dead—or the nearly dead. I asked her what she was talking about.

"Herbie's in the hospital, almost dead," she said. I wondered if hearing himself referred to as "Herbie" might finish off the little bastard. I also wondered what medical instruments they'd recently invented that could measure if something that had been born dead from the neck up was actually alive.

"What happened to him? Did his liver explode?"

"What's wrong with you, talking like that?" she asked.

"I don't care for Herbert T. Schwartz. I've never cared for Herbert T. Schwartz. And I don't much care if the Earth opens and swallows him, although I would feel sorry for the Earth's insides if it did."

I saw by my mother's expression that I was fighting a losing battle against one of those things mothers knew to be true in this world: You don't talk badly of the dead—or the nearly dead.

"Okay. Sorry, Mom. I *love* Herbert T. Schwartz, and I'm on a waiting list for a sex change operation so I can be his love slave and bear a dozen little Herbies and Herbiettes. So what's he nearly dead from? Inertia?"

"Those circus people jumped him and beat him over the head with a brick last night and he's in a coma and the doctors don't think he'll live."

I shrugged.

"And the mayor has told the circus to pack up and get out of town even though they were supposed to be here one more day."

The circus leaving town a day early seemed to be as much of a tragedy to my mother as Herbert T. Schwartz's mashed-in head. Tragedies to a mother raised Catholic are apparently judged only on the severity of their impact upon the household, and it is perfectly all right to lump different types of tragedies together so long as they are similarly devastating. "Margaret Tilko and I were going to go up to the circus tonight. We didn't get there last night, you know."

I hadn't known but I shrugged in understanding.

Before supper was over, Mrs. Leary from up the street called to tell my mother the latest. It wasn't the circus people who had done this terrible thing to little Herbie. Herbie had been drinking—well you know how he drinks, his poor mother. And two of the police officers who were patrolling the circus and who had it in for Herbie—they're jealous of him you know—beat him over the head with their nightsticks. And yes, my mother *did* ask if this meant that the circus could stay one more day. Mrs. Leary didn't know.

After supper, I called a guy I knew who was spending the summer working on the local newspaper. I asked him for the scoop on Herbert T. Schwartz. I knew I wasn't going to get the real story from anyone in East Mauch Chunk.

According to the information the newspaper had, after an earlier altercation with the Ferris-wheel operator, a progressively drunker Herbert T. Schwartz had come back (progressively drunker? How drunk can a guy get?), attempted to restart the fight that had been short-circuited earlier, and had passed out before anyone else arrived to join the fray. The Ferris-wheel operator dragged Herbert T. Schwartz over to the side of a truck and propped him against a tire to get him out of the way so he could continue operating the ride. This part of the story was confirmed by several people who were on the Ferris wheel at the time.

At 11:30, when the circus shut down for the night and the fireworks display began, the Ferris wheel operator and the guy from the ball-pitch stand decided to fix Herbert T. Schwartz's ass. They dragged him over, dropped him into one of the Ferris wheel cars, and sent it to the top. They then turned off the Ferris wheel and went to their truck to have a few brews before bed. And promptly forgot that Herbert T. Schwartz existed.

At some point between 11:30 and dawn the next morning when they found him sprawled below the Ferris wheel, Herbert T. Schwartz regained consciousness and, perhaps thinking he was going to stroll down the hall to the bathroom to take a piss, stepped out of the Ferris wheel car and dropped like a bunch of bananas to the straw-strewn ground below. He landed on his head, broke his neck, and mashed those parts of the brain theoretically having to do with cognitive thought. The two circus employees who'd put him up there were being held in county jail pending a hearing, and Herbert T. Schwartz was on permanent vacation at the hospital in Lehighton, his life hanging by a hair. And no, the circus would *not* be operating again tonight. On behalf of my mother and Mrs. Tilko, thanks a bunch, Herbert T.

Well, Herbert T. Schwartz's hair held, and after six and a half months in the "goober ward"—with two motorcycle hotshots who abhorred safely helmets as being uncool and a trio of teenage girls who felt that seatbelts did nothing more than wrinkle their dresses—and amidst mountains of medical bills, Herbert was taken home by his long-suffering mother so she could look after him. The hospital wasn't doing anything for him beyond janitorial functions anyway, and she could janitor him for a lot less money at home.

It should be noted again for the record that Herbert's twin from Hell, Randy, never went by to see Herbert's sorry ass, either at the hospital or at home on North Street.

As I now gather it, when the weather is tolerable, Herbert T. Schwartz's mother pushes him outside along the plywood wheelchair ramp she hammered together from the living room to the pavement against the expressed wishes of the East Mauch Chunk Zoning Commission. (The Schwartz house isn't zoned to permit a loading dock.) Mrs. Schwartz pushes Goober's wheelchair onto the grass between the pavement and the curb, between the struggling maple tree and the garbage can, so that Herbert can watch traffic go past. She checks up on him through the front window every few minutes to make certain he is alright because, apparently, not too many weeks after she began this practice back in the spring of 1968, some kids coming home from school—the Catholic school which Herbert had attended with such distinction and devotion—began pushing Herbert down the sidewalk.

When Mrs. Schwartz caught up to them, out of breath and about to blow a gasket, she asked them just what in God's name they thought they were doing taking Herbert. One of the boys said that they were playing with him; they thought he'd been put out at the curb to be taken away by the garbage man and they felt there was still some mileage left in him and that old wheelchair, so why waste it?

They thought the wheelchair "still had some mileage left in it." That's precious. See what a conservationist a Catholic education will make of you? They thought they'd recycle Herbert T. Schwartz and his old wheelchair. Jesus! Subsequent litters of parochial school kids are even dumber than we were.

Jack maneuvered the MGB around the corner at First and Center, pushed it up the hill in second gear, rattled along for four blocks, and hung another left, powered up again, stopped at the stop sign at North Street, ground out another left in first gear, and let the straining engine hold the car back as we lurched down the hill. He applied the brakes in a reassuring screech and we ground to a halt in front of Herbert T. Schwartz. The little car idled like an overloaded washing machine.

Even from the low angle at which I was sitting in the sports car, I was on a level with Herbert's drooping head. His face hung like a withered pear less than two feet away.

A string of drool hung off the corner of his slack mouth and I could distinctly hear his breathing, as though he'd just finished a two-mile run after a lifetime of smoking three packs of Marlboros a day. His teeth were gray and brown and even in the fresh October air, a dankness hung like crypt-breath along the two feet of open air separating our faces.

I looked up into his recessed eyes, which were shadowed by his brows and by the angle at which his head hung. There were two little reflections, indirect sunlight bouncing off what appeared to be opaque, dark-colored irises with no whites. Something set well back into the eyes seemed to hint at a flicker of life. Herbert's forehead furrowed and a sound came out of the deep tunnel of his throat, a sound like a bleat or a muffled scream. It was difficult to be precise about the sound as it strained against the ragged exhaust of Jack's car.

"Herbert, you prick," I said, "how are you?"

I didn't know what else to say. I felt sorry for this thing that was nearly human, because I'd been raised to feel guilty for those struck down in life and those less fortunate. But that upbringing arm-wrestled with the thousand slaps to the side of my head Herbert had administered through my eight years of parochial school—and with the memory of a child's fortune in Halloween candy rotting in the rain, and the knowledge that if the situation were reversed, Herbert's response would be to tip over my wheelchair or to undo the brake and send me careening down North Street while he laughed.

A bubbling dollop of drool dripped from the corner of Herbert's mouth. I imagined each bubble holding a word Herbert T. Schwartz was attempting to utter. Another sound issued from the deep tunnel behind his mouth, a sound like "Aaaaaaauuuuuughhh?!"

I extended myself a few inches closer, peering into Herbert's wrinkled face, and looked for some decipherable message—anything. At that moment, the withered head on its turkey neck lolled backwards and his eyes were suddenly out from under the shadows. The pupils were unusually huge, brown, rimmed with an imprecise dull blue, their very size pushing the whites away into his head. I had expected some remnant of the fires of hell that Herbert had always exuded. But there was nothing. Absolutely, positively nothing—just a big . . . nothing.

"Let's get outta here," Jack said. "We're runnin' late as it is, 'en Goober ain't got nothin' important to say to nobody."

Jack wrestled the gear lever into first against linkage that protested with a loud *clang*. As he popped the clutch in a threshing of abused metal, the door of the house that had been home to Herbert T. Schwartz opened.

Jack revved the engine toward a redline it no longer had the guts to achieve, power-shifted, and we wrenched forward in a cloud of oily blue smoke, moving at ever increasing speed away from Herbert's personal little hell.

"I can't wait to blow out some of the carbon today," Jack said above the croak of the engine as he shifted to third. "Then we'll stop off for a few cold ones."

Somewhere in the file rooms of my memory, a drawer slid shut with a metallic clang louder than the gear linkage on Jack's car. Somewhere deep down inside, a little vacuum sucked itself into existence, a vacuum purged of revenge.

*Originally published in Carver Magazine, 2001.*

# The Death of Tarzan

Ellie Raab never questioned her life.

The late-in-life only daughter of a late-in-life only daughter, last child of a '40s Pennsylvania hard-coal miner, she had immuned herself to her mother and brothers except for the barest essentials of food, shelter, and secondhand clothing.

Nowadays we would jump to conclusions—that her rough-hewn and brawny father had physically and emotionally shortchanged, perhaps even abused her. For Ellie was neither a handsome nor accessible girl. She was a young girl weighed down by an excess of unused childhood.

It was not her father who denied her, but her mother, who fervently believed, in fact, that Ellie existed merely as an unfair test, a daily trial to a precise Christian family.

It was her father, a miner born many levels below the high station of Ellie's mother, who loved his daughter and found in her existence his simple life's most elevated brush with heaven.

Where Ellie's mother found her an inconvenience and an abomination that should never have been born, Ellie's father found her late arrival an unanticipated boon, a reward for a life if not well-led (for Howard Raab was a modest man) at least well-intentioned. For him she promised all things for which he elevated women. Even on particularly difficult days at the mine, short-handed and dangerous, desperately in need of the maximum amount of calories to keep him tall and strong against the circumstances of a heart-pilfering job, he devoured his lunch from his tin lunchbox along with his grimed fellows, but ate it only halfway.

His unworthy grimed fingers carefully and reverently rewrapped one-half of his coarse summer sausage and orange-cheese sandwich in its waxed-paper vestments so that he could return it safely and unsullied to his Ellie. All else he ate and drank with ravenous enthusiasm, his strong tea with a touch of milk, the leftover cake with icing sticking to the waxed paper, the bruised apple—devouring the core and all. But the sandwich, no. His Ellie always sliced the sandwich precisely and carefully across the exact center. He carefully rewrapped it to preserve its freshness of spirit and intent.

He did not replace the sacred half-sandwich in his lunch pail. For if he had, there was a chance it would be intercepted and wrenched away by a member of his brood of sons, for they were as likely to knock over his rough, worn, scarred black lunchbox and squash its contents underfoot as they were to fail to acknowledge his intrusion into their midst after he stripped to the waist on the hottest or coldest day of the year to wash himself at the hose bib on the corner of the crumbling two-and-a-half-story house before coming inside. They were a wild bunch—the boys—undisciplined the day long by their mother, rebellious in collusion with her against their scarred father.

It was a conjugal moment in the long-shadowed shank of the afternoon when Ellie's father would lumber into the house, bump against her, and slip into the big pocket of her long, stained, shapeless housedress the holy host of the sandwich redeemed from the hellhole of the mine.

Silent as a ghost, Ellie would accept the half-sandwich like the lateral of a football from quarterback to halfback, and sprint for the attic, the aerie dungeon of her disgruntled mother's glorious past, where she would deposit it lovingly atop all the others her father had pressed into her keeping for the past five or six years. The pyramid of waxed-paper-wrapped half-sandwiches was very high, nearly to the peaked ceiling. She found it necessary to go up on her tiptoes to reach the top.

She knew by heart the date and the weight of each and every one of them. And as the half-sandwiches disintegrated over years, those on top compacting those on the bottom while time and decay sped the process, there was always another to be stacked on top to keep the pyramid tall. The first impression would be that the stench of so much meaty dissipation in every phase of the spectrum of rot would have made the attic unbearable. But the stench was stunted by some strange atmospheric dementia sealed in the attic, a sort of hermetically turbo-dry pyramid in which all was preserved, if imperfectly, yet preserved not in a pool of slime but rather in a petrifaction or desiccation.

Ellie spent much of her young life in the attic. The others knew that she spent her time there, but they never bothered to crawl up there themselves, as though strict invisible soldiers devoted to Ellie guarded its trapdoor. Or perhaps it was because the boys were just too damned lazy to make the climb.

In the attic, Ellie fingered the dust from the top surfaces of boxes and bundles and crates laboriously set there when her mother left her comfortable life to take up with Howard the miner, a calculated affront to her own mother, an appeal to her dying father, a fate beneath her high state that she stayed resigned to through a sort of galloping inertia.

As though the lives in families were carved deep into carbon paper, her relationship with Ellie was as noncommittal as her own mother's had been to her. And in the same way her own father's love for her had been nearly intense enough to compensate for the lack of motherly love, Howard's special love for Ellie smolderingly infuriated Ellie's mother as her mother must have been infuriated by what she had once referred to as the "sickly" relationship between her and her father.

Yet in spite of the void between mother and daughter, Ellie loved to stroke the boxes and bales that held the woman her mother had been before she'd gone and done that awful thing where she'd had to marry Howard Raab—only to learn, Ellie had heard from a gossiping aunt, that the sentence had been commuted by nature, but too late along the process for Ellie's mother to retrace her steps from marriage.

Ellie's grandmother had never forgiven Ellie's mother. The wrinkled frightening skeletal old woman still occasionally came to life long enough to remind Ellie's mother of the whole terrible series of misbegotten events. "You killed your father by the terrible thing you did!" the old lady would shout.

"He was already dead, thanks to you," Ellie's mother would respond. "You killed him before I was born."

Ellie stood for hours at the dirty attic windows, staring at the outside world from her roost. She watched the pigeons that strolled and strutted across the roof ledges, cooing and shitting, shitting and cooing. Like the people who lived on the other side of the window, people you couldn't trust, who would coo at you while they shat on your shoes. People walked by the house on the tree-lined street below— lots of people, for the house was just one block off the main street of the decaying dirty little coal town scabbed onto the side of Bear Mountain. Sometimes people who were passing looked at the house and pointed.

It kept Ellie sad to watch the pigeons socializing, to watch the people strolling back and forth, to feel as much as to hear vaguely, dimly from downstairs the running back and forth of her jackal brothers, their mother oblivious to them, oblivious to everything but her proud sorrow.

Her mother, Ellie knew, hated her, and if there were a way she could get away with it, Ellie was certain that her mother would kill her and bury her in the cellar, the always-locked cellar. She'd come so late in life, like a plague. Her mother wouldn't care at all if she were run over by a truck, flattened like a lame cat. In fact she would be glad. Her mother probably wouldn't even know Ellie was dead maybe for a week or two, she paid so little attention to her—except that then she, her mother, would have to make supper for the family by herself. It would be her poor father who would be the first to notice, to notice that Ellie wasn't there waiting behind the pantry door to receive the half-sandwich offering.

If her mother died before she did, Ellie would open the boxes and crates, and study her mother's other life to search for clues to why she was like she was. Ellie vaguely looked forward to that dusty day.

But until that day, the crates of her mother's life remained sealed. As did the waxed-paper-wrapped sandwich offerings her father presented to her that piled into the would-be-but-wasn't-putrid pyramid, dried out like thousands of little mummies. Ellie sometimes imagined her mother laid out in her very rich coffin, putrid inside, a crockpot of internal organs, on the outside desiccated like an Egyptian mummy. Like her grandmother, only dead and quiet, the mouth forever stilled, its pointed tongue dulled—its lashing forever leashed.

Ellie executed her homework in the attic, using boxes and crates of her mother's previous life as bench and desk, working feverishly under the 20-watt light bulb that hung bare on a twisted wire that dropped from a ceramic attachment in the peaked ceiling, rushing to get as much work behind her as was humanly possible before her sensitive fingers picked up the slim vibrations of the water rushing through the hose bib on the corner of the house, the signal that her father was home.

At the sound, Ellie would rush across the dusty room in such a flurry that clouds of motes would rise behind her usually limp but now fluttering plain dress, spooking the pigeons outside the dirty windows into a flurry of wings and loosened feathers, snapping off the dim bulb as she rushed for the returning stairs of the trapdoor. She moved like the ghost she'd trained herself to become—soundless, floating above the worn oaken floorboards, never causing a ripple or a creak. She flowed down the narrow stairs like water retreating to the sea along a flat beach, her breath held in anticipation, her apprehension unnecessary. For she was, after all, the only creature in the house who acknowledged or awaited her father's return from the mines. There was no competition.

She always, always reached the pantry door well before her father lumbered through the back-porch door into the dimly lit kitchen where her mother kept the blinds drawn against sunlight and what she considered jealous and overly curious neighbors. Ellie stood perfectly silent, as though a great bear had forced its way into the house after a particularly long hibernation, looking for something luscious to eat whole. The act of hiding, the anticipation of following the slow steps of her one and only father as he moved slowly through the long, narrow kitchen, thrilled her, made her nearly faint. She closed her eyes and forced her dead blue eyes to turn on their X-ray power like the Superman in her brothers' comic books so she could follow his every step.

He paused, he always paused, in the middle of the always deserted kitchen to extract the grayed handkerchief from the bottomless pocket of his worn heavy coat. There he would blow his nose once, twice, to expel the mucous rife with fine black greasy coal dust. Like a great bear blowing its nose open after hibernation to clear it so that it could better smell—so that it could better locate its necessary prey before devouring it and, by that act, begin again to live.

Ellie had learned in biology class that the bear's sense of smell is many thousands of times more fine than its sense of taste, which in its turn is many times more fine than its sight, which is not good at all. Her father squinted like a bear, refused to wear the dime-store spectacles she'd bought him for Christmas except when she insisted. The bear blew its nose once, twice. She could see him through the solid wall carefully refold the handkerchief and move slowly toward the pantry door, past which he'd walk in slow motion on his way to the living room.

Like the ghost she was, Ellie flowed from behind the pantry door and, as her father always did, he feigned surprise at encountering her. He smiled his weary smile, not showing his gray teeth. She could smell the dankness of the mine on his heavy, unwashed coat. It smelled of deep, dark, dirty places where men beat themselves to death against rock. And inside the envelope of dirt and chill, her father radiated his own slow furnace. She thrilled at the mountain of sensations that assailed her.

She wrapped herself around him for a moment, the aroma of coal dust thick and overwhelming, the envelope of chill she penetrated sparking electric—the core of warmth she briefly touched exhilarating. Her father lightly touched the top of her head with a rough paw, patted her gently, and then moved just as gently to break the contact. The bear lived in fear of being found out, of the consequences of loving his daughter too well.

His paw slipped into the big pocket of his rough coat and came out with the carefully wrapped half-sandwich. In a motion both gentle and mechanical, he slipped the sandwich into the deep pocket of Ellie's shapeless dress, shrugged himself out of the heavy coat, hung it on a peg behind the pantry door, and moved away toward the dark parlor. The boys were outside somewhere, roughhousing, breaking things.

Ellie stood still, watching the retreating back of her father, so big and strong and yet seemingly so wounded. The half-sandwich in her deep pocket radiated its warmth like a newborn puppy, and her father at this moment always seemed as vulnerable.

She stood still for many minutes behind the pantry door, allowing herself to cool down to what passed for normal.

She lived for this moment, and had for as long as she could remember. The icebox, her mother's latest extravagance, whirred from around the corner in the kitchen. Somewhere in the house, a floorboard creaked. Muffled sounds of children screeching as they ran down the street out front filtered through. And there was the muted sound of the obligatory conversation going on in the parlor between her mother and father, most of the conversation coming in her mother's low voice.

Ellie almost daily toyed with the idea of creeping near the parlor doorway in an attempt to overhear them, but the fear of the imagined—and, she felt, the guaranteed—punishment by her mother if she were caught was too overwhelming to her, a wall she could not imagine forcing herself over.

Instead she stood quietly, picking up no words, only the low hum of speech too far away to decipher. Her mother did not scream or rant. That was not her mother. Her mother spoke quietly but forcefully. The most her mother ever raised her voice was when she and her own mother confronted each other. At those times, all propriety was savagely shredded. Ellie was always dragged along whenever her mother confronted her own mother. The boys were allowed to do as they pleased, and it never pleased them to visit their grandmother, except on Christmas Eve when the visit earned them a present.

Ellie silently made her way up the steps to the attic where she carefully placed the fresh sandwich atop the pyramid. She now had a half-hour in which to finish whatever homework she'd been unable to rush through earlier. Then she would need to help her mother prepare supper while her father read the newspaper in the parlor. It was Tuesday. The meal would be vegetable soup and dumplings.

She lost herself in the required reading she loved, the required reading most of her classmates despised. She knew she was in line to read out loud the next morning. She knew that she was ready with her lesson, and just as surely she knew that she would freeze up when it came time for her to slide out of her seat, force herself to stand, and hear the words expelled like pebbles from a swollen mouth that was no longer under her control. She would hold the book open at her navel, hold it so desperately perfectly parallel to the oak plank floor that equal plumb lines dropped from each corner of the book would dance like ballerinas. Her face would be hidden within the spider webs of her ratty dun hair, and she would monotonously plod and blunder through a world that this afternoon she found filled with light and love and wonder. She would suffer her sentence and bear the "That's good, Ellisia" from Sister Mary Joseph. She would slide back into her seat, slide her open book carefully onto her desktop, and check out of the real world for the rest of the class.

She would check out of the world for the rest of her life. She would check out of the world. Out of the world for the rest of her life. Her life . . .

A bang at the bottom of the retractable stairs leading to her attic aerie startled her. "Hey, Dimwit, yo, get your sorry butt downstairs. The old lady wants ya," her brother Donald called up the stairs. "Get on it! I'm hungry!" He bashed his hand against the bottom stair again, startling Ellie as effectively as though she had not heard him the first time.

Ellie ranged her eyes around the dingy attic as though contemplating foreign landscapes at twilight. She blinked herself awake, closed her book, turned off the dim bulb, and silently flowed down the stairs. At the bottom, she tucked the toe of her worn brown shoe under the lip of the lowest step, nudged it, and it rose on its springs to accordion together, the whole apparatus folding itself neatly into the ceiling. She held it back, controlled its ascension by playing out the line that hung from the trapdoor.

She poured herself down the stairs to the first floor and marched herself to the kitchen, taking care to make some sound on the bare planks with her heavy shoes so as not to startle her mother. She pulled her apron from a peg behind the pantry door, three pegs over from her father's heavy coat. She brushed the back of her right hand along the rough sleeve of his coat as she turned away to enter the kitchen.

Her mother sat on a stool, as she usually did, a cup of lukewarm tea with lemon slice and honey in front of her, and directed Ellie's vivisectioning of celery, carrots, cucumber, and cabbage. Ellie's mother oversaw the process in a used, bored manner, sipping her tea with dull resignation, reciting to Ellie the steps necessary to make the soup that Ellie had long since tattooed onto her autonomic system. She worked in a dream, each movement seemingly underwater, slow and precise, deliberate and robotic. She could hear her brothers carrying on upstairs. Her mother made no sign she heard a thing. The monotonous click of the teacup on the worn wooden table came like slaps of thunder. Between the numbing racket, Ellie listened for the occasional sweet crisp crinkle of her father in the front room turning a page of the newspaper. The occasional crinkling sound caused her to just as occasionally smile under her breath.

In the way a dental surgery patient slips along a great highway of time and turns it into a mere pathway through the help of nitrous oxide, Ellie slipped through her labors. The soup warmed, heated on the open flame, then simmered. The sound of her brothers running through the rooms on the second floor dulled, her mother's instructions drummed like rain on a tin roof, the dumplings came together, the table was set, and as the moment to call her brothers to supper approached, the shields clanged into place around Ellie.

She sipped her soup in the middle of the maelstrom that whirled around her, vaguely felt Herbie grab her hair and pull, just as vaguely heard her father protest, their mother's "they're just being boys," saw the tablespoon making a trip to the bowl to fill with gray vegetable soup then rise to her lips then empty then return over and over, then the rush from the table, a vacuum sucking everything from the kitchen except Ellie and the disarray of dirty dishes and pots.

Ellie kept a copy of Thrilling Wonder Stories hidden under a loose board in the attic. She dreamed of living on a spaceship rushing toward a distant planet, its airlock stuffed with her brothers, her finger on the control that would open the outer hatch that would allow the grand vacuum of outer space to suck her brothers to its cold bosom. The story with the airlock didn't use the words "to its cold bosom," but Ellie filled in with those words. "To its cold bosom"—Puff! Gone. Goodbye, Donald; goodbye, Herbie; goodbye, Rudy. See you somewhere out beyond Saturn, maybe.

She smiled as she cleared the table, ran the hot water into the sink, sloshed the water around, cleaned and dried the dishes, and slowly and meticulously brought the kitchen back to order. She skulked into the parlor, where everyone else was gathered. "What took you so long?" her mother demanded. "You did well," her father said from the shadows where his pipe glowed a bing-cherry red.

Her mother glared into the shadows, but dared say nothing during this holy evening ritual. The Bible lay open on her lap. She began to read in her low, menacing voice, the three boys scrootching around trapped in their places on the long sofa, the only time during a twenty-four-hour period when their mother demanded their transformation from assassins to saints.

Ellie heard the words her mother read from the Bible, heard each and every one of them, and followed the story the words built, but followed nothing of what they meant. In another compacting of the time thoroughfare, the session was over. Her brothers blasted off the sofa and were gone in a wild roar like the launch of a German V-2 rocket. Ellie attempted to fade away from the room, successfully avoiding detection by her mother. Her mother seemed intent on their father.

Ellie carefully climbed the stairs as quietly as possible—which, for her, was very quiet. She did not return to her attic. She flowed down the hall to the cubbyhole of her bedroom and closed the door nearly all the way, hoping her brothers would forget she existed. She pulled her math text off the pile of schoolbooks and began to scratch out the remainder of her homework.

She finished and dozed a bit. She woke to her father's heavy footsteps coming up the stairs. He loomed in her doorway, filled her little room, radiated the heat he carried deep within himself. He lowered himself ponderously to the single bare wooden chair and nodded at her labored figures. "Homework," he said simply. "Always homework." He sighed, not for her, but for himself, for his own homework left undone.

"Are you ready for a story?" he asked, same as he did every night at this time. Ellie closed her math book, leaving her pencil stub and her worksheet inside to mark the page. As she did every night at this time, Ellie nodded her head vigorously.

"Which one?" her father asked.

"Tarzan," Ellie gushed.

Her father began, "In a little Slovakian village, a scrawny little boy played with his scrawny little cat."

"What color was the cat?" Ellie asked, as she always did.

"It was a black cat with white paws and a white mustache," her father said, as he always did.

"All the other boys in the village picked on this little boy," Ellie's father continued. "All the dogs in the village picked on this little cat. One day, a pack of the village curs . . ."

"Curs," Ellie whispered under her breath.

". . . a pack of the village curs caught and killed the little cat—so badly that there wasn't anything left of it for the little boy to bury. The little boy buried the memory of his little cat and then cried for two days over the loss of his only friend. When he finally stopped crying, he realized that while he had been occupied with his crying, the half of his brain that was not crying was very angry and was busy formulating a plan.

"Now this was the scrawny little boy's plan: he would go into the woods for one hour every day after school, and each day he would find a rock bigger than the one he found the day before, and he would walk around his little clearing carrying that rock and raising it above his head again and again and again. And when the hour was finished, he would set the rock down on the ground, lining up the rocks around the clearing.

"The first month he crawled home exhausted, barely able to open his mouth to sip the broth at the supper table. But eventually he became very good at lifting and carrying rocks."

"He became proficient," Ellie said, having learned that word that day in school.

"Yes," her father said, "he became very proficient."

And so the story went. Ellie had heard this one a dozen times before, but she listened to it, rapt. In her cramped little bedroom, she drank in the warmth and the closeness of her wonderful father—so wonderful that her little cubbyhole of a room felt like its own huge planet swimming through a wonderfully peaceful warm nothingness.

"The little boy's parents immigrated to America and, after using his well-earned strength to assert himself in his new neighborhood, in his new school, surviving the initiation rites all outsiders go through before they are accepted in a new and strange place, the young boy graduated from the sisters' school and began to work in the mines where his prodigious strength earned him the nickname Tarzan. He became known to everyone as Tarzan until no one even remembered his given name. He could even lift a telephone pole all by himself. Any young man who can do that deserves to be called Tarzan," he said.

"Years passed. Tarzan prospered in the hard life of the coal mines. He married and had three children, none of whom was named Tarzan Junior because, being Tarzan's children, they did not have to learn to defend themselves. But eventually, like many miners, Tarzan contracted black lung disease from all the coal dust he breathed in over all the years. And, little by little, and then more swiftly, the mighty Tarzan became weakened, and he shrunk and could no longer go into the mines. And he turned into a scrawny little old man, forty-two-years old, who did not have the strength to lift a matchstick. (This was a man who once could lift telephone poles all by himself.)

"Everyone loved and respected Tarzan because, even though he had mighty strength, he never took advantage of it to hurt anyone in the little town. Always remembering his little cat, he was also kind to animals—and to his children. But even to the day he died, he was known as Tarzan, for no one even remembered his given name. And years after his death, they still speak of Tarzan as though at any minute he is likely to come striding around a corner, a telephone pole slung over his shoulder."

Her father gently removed the mathematics book from Ellie's stilled hands, carefully folded her hands on her chest, and raised the blanket until it covered her to her neck. He quietly laid the book on the chair he'd occupied, then bent over Ellie to kiss her forehead before turning off the weak light. He crept out of the little room and closed the door all the way except for a little crack that allowed the light from the hallway to act as a nightlight.

He heard the boys, at the other end of the house, chasing each other, but the level of their activity was beginning to run down. The world was slowing. He went downstairs and sat in the front room smoking his pipe and seemingly reading a book while his wife sat across from him, darning by rote one of the boys' socks. Neither spoke. At 9:30, they removed themselves from their chairs and went through the door to their separate beds in the front bedroom.

Ellie's next day was muddied. At school, she was assailed by the gray spot of her recitation—overwhelmed by it, sullied by it. She had missed only one answer in her mathematics homework, but that little triumph was outweighed by the gray blob of her recitation. At recess, Kathy Tierman told her she had done well. But Kathy Tierman, desperate for a friend, told everyone they did well. At the end of the school day, Ellie ran home and began her routine, a safe place to be, at least "safe" as she knew it.

Ellie executed her homework in the attic, the boxes and crates of her mother's life serving as bench and desk. She worked feverishly under the bulb that lost the battle with the day's grayness. She became uncomfortable and then agitated when her sensitive fingers failed to feel the pulse of the water running out to the hose bib where her father should be washing up before coming inside.

But today something was amiss. She desperately wanted her father to lift the grayness. She wanted to wallow in the anticipation, when he put her to bed, of relating to him the events of her day at school.

But the gray day was wrong.

The shadows that crept onto her through the dirty windows were wrong. They were too long; they were shadows of a later day, a worn-out day. She cocked her ear to catch the sound of her mother and father moving about downstairs, certain she'd somehow become engrossed in her homework to the point that she hadn't heard the water rushing through the old pipe on the side of the house as her father washed the coal dirt from his face and hands before entering the kitchen.

Her brothers were outside somewhere, roaming the hillside, inflicting destruction. The quiet was awful; it made her nervous. Her fingers played with themselves. They should have felt the vibrations of the old water pipe by now.

She walked to the low dirty windows looking out over the street out front just as a big dark green car pulled up. Cars never pulled up front at their house. A man weighed down with a Sunday hat and a topcoat—she couldn't see who it was—got out and walked to the front door. Nobody ever came to the front door; they always used the side door, just like everyone else in town. Ellie could hear the insistent knocking at the front door. The doorbell hadn't worked in years; it had rusted itself mute.

She blinked the lowering sun from her eyes, turned and flew to her pyramid of degenerating sandwiches, roughly grabbed the top one off the pile, tore it from its waxed paper envelope, and shoved it into her mouth and ate it. She snatched another, then another, desperate to again be a part of Tarzan's world.

# Ellie's Brothers

It was only by chance that Herbie glanced down the steep mountainside. Donald and Rudy, his older and younger brothers, had leaned back into truck-sized boulders when "Time out! Goddamn time out!" had been called by Donald during the stone-throwing war that raged every weekday after school and all day Saturday on the west flank of Bear Mountain. Instead of joining his sweating brothers, Herbie had plopped down on his stomach on a flat rock, facing downhill toward town, licking the blood off the back of his hand where Donald had scored a hit.

The leafless trees did not obscure his view, although the little coal-mining town below seldom drew his attention once he had escaped the confines of their ratty house. That dump was a weary two-and-a-half–story, beaten-up faux-Victorian on a narrow little lane scabbed onto the mountain's shoulder, across the ravine from the main town of East Mauch Chunk. The sad house was out of their minds as soon as they charged uphill, where they crossed into their wild-Indian territory.

It was an honest-to-goodness genuine accident that Herbie glanced down that day; his mother would later call it providence. But as his brothers excitedly argued back and forth about who was winning the rock-throwing war, their blood fast and hot with passion—twigs thrown back and forth like exclamation points following "Did so!" "Did not!"

"Did so!" "Did not!"—Herbie watched a long, green, four-door sedan pick its way carefully along the broken asphalt of Ash Street, all four blocks of it.

To this day he can't explain from where the lousy feeling of certainty came, as it ascended like a methane-filled balloon from his stomach, but he knew, he knew that sedan was going to pull up in front of 37 Ash Street—their house.

He followed the car's careful progress, wishing his father could afford to buy a luxury sedan like that (hell, any car), still willing it to stop in front of their rundown monstrosity of a house.

Please, he whispered to himself, closing his eyes tightly, clenching his fists to increase the pressure on whoever up there was in charge of arranging such things. Meanwhile, behind him, the laboriously negotiated ceasefire fractured as Rudy spit at Donald to make his point even more perfectly clear.

"Sssssssshhhhhhhhh!" Herbie hissed at them—unfortunately, not loud enough for the sound to wedge its way between the walls of warring factions.

The green sedan turned slowly toward the dead-grass lawn in front of the house, the slanting afternoon sun ricocheting off a strip of silvered chrome that ran along the front fender. "It's a Packard," Herbie said to himself as the level of chaos behind him ratcheted up. "It's a goddamned Packard," he said. The only person who owned a Packard in East Mauch Chunk was Mr. Harrison C. Tremont, the vice president and general manager of the Black Sparrow Mine, where his father worked.

"Mr. Tremont must be coming to dinner," Herbie

thought. "He's never done that before. Nobody's ever done that before."

Mr. Tremont carefully helped himself from behind the steering wheel of his luxury Packard and walked slowly up the steps to their front porch. Behind Herbie, Rudy called Donald a "goddamned liar."

"Not!" Donald shot back.

"Are!" Rudy said.

Mr. Tremont paused before pressing the doorbell.

"No! It don't work!" Herbie shouted without thinking. "Ya gotta bang on the door!"

"What?" Donald asked from behind him.

The sound of battle had ceased. A bitter breeze roamed across the barren mountainside. "What the hell's goin' on?" Donald asked, making his way down to Herbie's perch.

Herbie pointed toward the house as a bristle of wind blew a wave of browned leaves and dust among them, stinging their eyes.

After two attempts to rouse someone inside the house by using the doorbell, Mr. Tremont concluded that it didn't work and rapped solidly but hesitantly on the big door. Two-and-a-half stories above him, a blotch of white the texture of tapioca moved past the dirty window and was gone.

"Ellie . . ." Herbie muttered under his breath.

"What?" Donald asked.

"Ellie," Herbie said. "Ellie was at the window." Something like an oncoming stomachache pulled at his guts.

"She's always at the window," Rudy said. "She's a waste of window." Rudy picked up a fist-sized stone and tossed it half-heartedly downhill, pleased with his talent to sum up the situation in a few words.

"Ellie . . ." Herbie repeated. Donald hit him hard on the arm.

"Enough Ellie, already," Donald said.

Below them the door of their house slowly opened and Mr. Tremont removed his hat and lowered his head and spoke to someone within the shadows. He nervously, slowly spun his hat in his hands. Then he lowered his head and walked away.

The door slammed shut with enough force that a second after it closed, the three of them could hear it all the way up on the mountainside. The sound caused Mr. Tremont to pause before descending the front steps. He replaced his hat, pulled it down far enough to shadow his eyes, and slowly returned to his car. He lowered himself into the plush front seat and slowly closed the big door. And then just sat there, staring ahead.

"Poor Ellie," Herbie said.

"Poor Ellie," Donald parroted, again hitting Herbie a good one on his upper arm. "Let's get the hell outta here." He jumped up and began walking uphill. "Let's get our asses up to Big Rock then run down the other side of the mountain."

Herbie looked up at Donald, who vibrated like a wind-up alarm clock going off. He wanted out of there.

Behind him, the dark clouds above the mountain formed a horizontal slit, and for a moment a strip of blue sky peeked through. A second later the slit had vanished.

"Hey, look, there's old Mr. Ferko," Rudy said, pointing off to the downside of the street. Mr. Ferko had once been a lumbering elephant of a man, and had played tackle for the Philadelphia Eagles a decade earlier. He walked with a limp, his miner's clothes a uniform gray, making him almost invisible against the gray street.

After leaving the mine on Mt. Pisgah across the river, the Black Sparrow miners crossed the bridge, ambled down to the Lehigh Valley Railroad station, across the parking lot, and up the wooden steps toward their homes on Pleasant Hill on the low side of Bear Mountain.

As Mr. Ferko reached the front of their house, he stopped for a moment and doffed his formless hat, running a rough hand through his thinning hair. Herbie had seen a picture of a statue in a book last year in the library; it was called "The End of the Journey" or something like that. A tired, dejected Indian warrior sat on the back of a tired, worn-down horse. Mr. Ferko looked like the tired, worn-down horse. He frequently spit out big black lungers the size of small toads, and each year he got thinner and people said he wouldn't last too much longer from developing Black Lung. He slowly pulled his hat back on and shuffled on his old bones down the street to his own gray house.

Just reaching the top of the steps was Mr. Lennon, a small, brisk man who today walked as though wearing cinder blocks for shoes.

Usually the miners came home in groups of three or four, talking, telling dirty jokes, and tiredly punching each other in the upper arm to make a point. The boys were so used to the adult male gesture of punching someone's arm that they had made it one of their own gestures of punctuation. But now the men worked their way up the hill like the thinned-out end of a parade of exhausted ants returning to their anthill.

Donald grabbed Herbie's sleeve and pulled at him.

"Let's get out of here," he repeated, pulling next at Rudy, eager to go uphill, to defy gravity, to get away from whatever it was below them that was making him uneasy. Rudy pulled against him; feeling his own need to go downhill, with gravity, to return to their house to find out what was going on.

Their father's fellow miners continued to slog uphill toward home, a broken line of used-up zombies.

Rudy looked back and forth between Herbie and Donald as though torn between the two, wanting one or the other to prevail so he wouldn't feel so uncertain, so the decision to go up or down wouldn't be his. A few big drops of rain fell among them, pulling their attention away from each other. The promise of rain seemed to settle the tug of war. Donald let go of Herbie's sleeve and sluggishly led the three of them downhill, kicking stones out of the way as he went, walking as slowly as possible without outright stopping.

The miners continued to slog on past their house, one of them occasionally glancing furtively at the gray brooding monstrosity. There was no more evidence of Ellie in the dirty attic window. The house was as quiet as a dead bug.

Until the boys got closer.

When they reached the far side of the street, they began to hear a thin keening, like wind rubbing against telephone lines. The sound stopped them in their tracks.

Mr. Gillespie trudged past them. He touched the brim of his hat and said, "Boys," then moved on. His face was streaked with black coal dust and his eyes glistened. He seemed not to hear the strange sound coming from their unpainted house. Mr. Gillespie was a bit hard of hearing anyway.

The boys stood in the middle of the street, not eager to

approach the strange sound. They looked back and forth at each other, hoping that one of them would make some sort of a move, either to continue on home or to flee into the mountain.

Another handful of large raindrops fell among them and the damp breeze picked up speed. Herbie used it as an excuse to break the deadlock. To prevent himself from changing his mind, he ran across what remained of the street and around the side of the house so he could come in through the back door. (The front door and the vestibule beyond it were closed to them.) He found himself humming "A Frog Went A-Courtin'" in an attempt to cover the sound coming from inside the house. Donald and Rudy followed him, slower and less enthusiastically.

Arriving at the back steps, Herbie ran up them two at a time, making as much noise as his clodhoppers could manage, sending a signal ahead that they were coming. The keening sound—louder, now that he was closer—didn't change. Its owner either didn't hear them coming or didn't care.

Herbie grabbed the doorknob and was about to turn it when Donald grabbed his hand. Donald shook his head "No" but Herbie turned it anyway.

As he pushed the door open, the sound doubled in volume, rushing at them like a troop of banshees, standing the hairs on the backs of their necks straight out. It was obvious as soon as they were inside that the sound was coming from their parents' bedroom. And it was obvious to them which of their parents was wailing.

They pushed through the coatroom and the kitchen and into the dining room, where the closed drapes made the heavy furniture look like blocks of dark granite. The

closer they moved to the bedroom door, the more the keening seemed to coalesce into something more substantial, im-
peding their progress, pushing them back.

When they at last stood in front of the closed door, they
felt as though they had been attacked and beaten with a baseball bat. Their legs felt weak. Donald continued to shake his
head, both against what they were doing and in an attempt
to keep the eerie sound from getting any further into his
ears. Rudy held his hands over his ears, but that did little to
muffle the sound. It came in waves, their mother taking a
breath only when her lungs were completely spent of air. The
sound never changed in pitch or volume. It was almost mechanical—the wailing sound, then a wet sucking sound, the
wailing sound, then more sucking noises as though someone
were drowning.

Herbie didn't attempt to open the door. He didn't touch
the doorknob. He raised his fist and before he could change
his mind, he knocked hard on the heavy door.

The sound of the knock, enormously loud to them, was
seemingly lost under the weight of the wailing. The knock
didn't change the wailing in any way. It was as though the
knock fell into a deep well and was gone before it reached the
other side of the door.

Herbie knocked again, harder, but again nothing happened. Rudy began making a moaning sound, his hands still
covering his ears. Donald continued to shake his head back
and forth.

Before Herbie could knock a third time, Donald grabbed
his hand and pulled him away. He continued to shake his
head "No, no, no, no . . ."

Donald herded them upstairs to his bedroom and closed
the door against the horrible sound. It was worse than their

mother's long periods of mean silence that she regularly used in order to punish them. Rudy dropped into a corner, still holding his hands over his ears. Donald fell onto his bed, a weak moan slipping out of him. Herbie sat on the plain wooden chair; he held himself back from grinding his teeth as a way of distracting himself from the sound that now seemed to fill the world. He wondered if the neighbors heard it, or if God heard it.

"What're we gonna do?" Donald asked, slowly writhing on his bed.

"It can't go on forever," Herbie said. "She's gotta run out of steam sometime."

"Why's she doin' it?" Donald asked. "Just because Mr. Tremont came by? 'Cause he saw our dopey house?"

Herbie shook his head. He thought the keening was dropping in volume; he hoped he was right. "Mr. Tremont would've only come if he had bad news to deliver," Herbie said. "Something's happened to our father."

Donald sat up in his bed. "Like what?"

"I dunno," Herbie said. "Something. Something bad."

Rudy stayed wedged into the corner of the room, his hands still covering his ears.

"What're we gonna do?" Donald asked no one in particular. He crossed his arms as though he was cold. The high wailing continued to seep through the walls.

"What about Ellie?" Herbie asked.

"What about her?" Donald said.

"She's up in the attic. She knows something's wrong. She must be worried," Herbie said.

"She's never worried," Donald said. "She's like a bossy little old lady."

"A worried little old lady," Herbie said. With that, he

stood up from the chair, opened the door, and went out into the hallway. At the end of the hall was the access door to the attic set into the ceiling. The door and the folding wooden stairs were pulled up. The rope to pull the stairs down dangled just above his reach.

He went back into Donald's room, picked up the chair, and carried it into the hall. The piercing cries from below were especially bad there, as though they'd become amplified as they came up the stairs and bounced off the walls of the hall.

Donald came out into the hall, reluctantly, to see what Herbie was doing. A moment later Rudy stuck his head out the door, safely hiding behind Donald.

Herbie placed the chair under the recessed stairs, mounted the chair in a nonchalant leap, and grabbed the blue plastic ring at the end of the rope. Rudy ran out from behind Donald to get a better view.

Herbie tugged at the rope, ready to leap out of the way of the descending stairs. But nothing happened. He tugged again. Nothing. He looked at Donald. "She has it locked from inside," he said.

Donald ran forward, roughly pushed Herbie off the chair, and tugged at the rope himself. It didn't give an inch. "Shit!" he cried. "Open up! Open up, Ellie! Now!"

There was no sound from above. Even if there had been, it would have likely been drowned out by the banshee wail of their mother. Above the wailing, though, they heard faintly the sound of someone banging on the front door.

"You stay here—in case she opens it," Donald commanded. "I'll see who it is."

He leaped down the stairs three at a time, the crash of

his clodhoppers ricocheting off the walls. Herbie and Rudy could follow his heavy-footed progress through the dining room, into the parlor, and out into the vestibule. Their mother's wail continued its forty seconds of keening followed by five seconds of near-silence as she sucked in a new breath so she could start over again.

A few seconds later, Donald stuck his head around the corner. He waved at them to come downstairs. "It's Mr. and Mrs. Gillespie," he said. "They need to talk to us." He vanished back around the corner.

Rudy launched himself like a torpedo, going down the stairs two at a time, building speed as he went. Herbie followed more conservatively, hoping that Rudy made it safely around the corner. He did—barely.

When Herbie reached the parlor, the vestibule door and the front door were open and Mr. and Mrs. Gillespie were silhouetted against the gray outside world. For a moment— to Herbie, who occasionally read science-fiction books— their two bent-over, nondescript neighbors looked like a pair of wizened visitors from outer space.

Downstairs, this close to their parents' bedroom, their mother's wail was piercing, orange-colored.

The Gillespies motioned the three boys to come outside. The wind had picked up, knifing through the little hillside burg like damp specters from the cemetery. But the rain had stopped. Herbie didn't notice the chill.

"Where's your sister?" Mrs. Gillespie asked.

Donald pointed upwards. "In the attic, where she usually is."

Mrs. Gillespie nodded, as though she knew that all along. Without noticing that they were being herded away from their house, the boys walked down the stairs and out onto the street, where Mrs. Gillespie turned them toward the Gillespie house three doors away.

"Where're we goin'?" Rudy asked.

The couple exchanged a glance but marched on. "We're going by our house for a little while," Mrs. Gillespie said. "I sent Bobby to get the priest." Bobby was their only son, three years older than Donald, a halfback on the junior-varsity football team.

As they walked, the wind and the increasing distance muffled their mother's lamentations. Mrs. Gillespie looked back, like Lot's wife trying for a last glimpse of Gomorrah. "Poor woman," she muttered. Pulling herself closer together against the increasing wind, she didn't turn into a pillar of salt.

The Gillespies' house, unlike their own, was in a perpetual state of faux-remodeling. Mr. Gillespie fancied himself something of a handyman, which he clearly was, but he was also very much a half-hearted handyman. He began projects with a great burst of energy only to have it peter out several days or weeks later. His son Bobby followed in his wake: a demon in the first half of a football game, he seemed to lose interest once the half-time balling out by the coach was over. But the house, with all its quilt-like painting projects and repair efforts, was cozy, like a house in a fairy tale—all haphazard because the people inside were happy in all kinds of different ways. The exterior of the house, too, reflected that careless and all-encompassing patchwork happiness.

Mrs. Gillespie opened the back door. An aroma of cinnamon and mint and warmth rushed out as though it was becoming too much for the house to contain. Instead of having to push against the out-rushing warmth, the boys were pulled inside as though by a giant purring vacuum cleaner loaded with new baked goods.

This was the first time all three boys had been inside the Gillespie house at the same time. They occasionally came one at a time when it was the season to sell Christmas cards or Easter candy for the school, but then they only stood just inside the door, feeling uncomfortable in all that warmth and cupcake aroma.

The heat was obviously coming from the big, black, chrome-highlighted coal stove that took up most of one wall. An unfrosted chocolate cake sat on a pedestal on one side of the stove. Mrs. Gillespie had apparently been deep into working her bakery magic on the cake when Mr. Gillespie came home with the bad news from the mine.

Herbie realized suddenly that although he could intuit well enough that something had happened at the mine, and that it involved his father, nobody had explained to them exactly what had happened, what had broken the back of the afternoon for so many people.

The three boys stood just inside the now-closed kitchen door looking like a trio of Bowery urchins caught in a benign fairy tale. Somewhere in the house a cuckoo clock chirped that it was five o'clock.

Rudy stood to the side of and just a bit behind Donald. Herbie stood beside Donald and felt obliged to take a half step forward before he was allowed to speak. "Mr. Gillespie," he said quietly, "what's happened to our father?" He took a quick glance at Donald, who seemed to approve of his asking for some clarity. "Something's wrong and nobody's told us . . ."

Mr. Gillespie removed his tired hat and held it awkwardly in his dark, scarred hands, turning it slowly. "It's like this, boys," he said. "We . . . we had some trouble in the mine today . . . . Some shoring, old shoring gave way . . . and the ceiling, some of the ceiling, fell in. Just a bit, you see." He stole a long glance at his wife. "Your father, well . . ."

Rudy began to sniffle, suddenly aware of the implications.

Mrs. Gillespie rushed to Rudy and embraced him, engulfing him in her apron. The kindness of the move, so foreign to any of the boys, gave Rudy permission to cry openly. Donald issued a snarl at Rudy's weakness, but Herbie's fierce glance at him stopped it. It was the first time Herbie had ever seen Rudy cry. His usual response to something unpleasant was to whine until their mother made the unpleasantness go away.

Herbie felt a knot rise in his throat as Mr. Gillespie's stammering faded off. He didn't need to say anything else. "I'll be in the front room," he said to his wife, "having a little pipe." He turned slowly, embarrassed, and disappeared through the door.

Mrs. Gillespie stroked Rudy's hair while Donald and Herbie stood awkwardly, wanting to shuffle their feet, but holding them in check. The awkward moment was breached when they heard the heavy footsteps of Bobby Gillespie coming around the house.

With his customary enthusiasm he flung open the door and leaped in, bringing with him a rush of cold air. He quickly closed the door and removed his baseball cap, slapping it against his knee. "Father Szabo is at the house," he announced in a tone of voice a radio baseball broadcaster would use to declare that Richie Ashburn was stealing second base. Taller than his parents, Bobby was orange-haired and built like a greyhound.

"Whazzamatter with him?" he asked, nodding at Rudy.

"Bobby!" his mother said. "His father——"

"Oh, yeah," Bobby said, as though he hadn't just returned from running across town to summon the parish priest to the home of the deceased. "When're we gonna eat?" he said.

His mother gave him a hard look. "What?" he said. "Youse guys are hungry, I bet," he said to Donald and Herbie. Donald nodded on their behalf.

"Go in the dining room and set the table," Mrs. Gillespie said, still stroking Rudy's hair. He'd stopped crying and stood like a bundle of brooms leaning against Mrs. Gillespie's apron, his hands dead at his sides.

Bobby turned toward the door, then turned back and beckoned Donald and Herbie to come help him. As though released from a bad dream, the two followed Bobby through the door, glad to be away from Rudy's tears.

Bobby knelt down and fished six plates out from the bottom shelf of a cabinet backed against the wall. He handed them to Herbie, who set them around the big, heavy dining-room table. Bobby roughly pulled out a drawer—"Damned thing always sticks!" he said—and passed rough silverware to Donald.

The inside of the Gillespie house, although more colorful than their own, matched the exterior. Projects had been begun and then left unfinished. The cabinet from which Bobby had extracted the silverware had been sanded down on one side as though being prepped for painting, but had never felt the touch of a paint brush. One of the chairs pushed against the wall had been stripped of cane, and someone had begun to re-cane it, but had quit halfway through the process. But all in all, Herbie liked the place. The unfinished projects made it feel alive, so unlike his own house where everything just sort of sat, as though waiting for eternity to arrive.

When the table was set, Bobby led them into the parlor and motioned for them to sit down, as though the Gillespies used the parlor all the time.

Herbie looked around. There were a half-dozen copies of the local newspaper spread out on the coffee table as well as three copies of National Geographic and one VFW magazine, a pair of men's slippers casually resting against the side of a worn stuffed chair, and a pipe lying in an ashtray that had a half-inch of ash on the bottom. He sat next to Donald on the sofa while Bobby picked up the pipe and pretended that he was going to smoke it. Herbie could hear Mr. Gillespie moving around upstairs, making the floorboards squeak.

The room was heated by a pair of logs burning lazily in the big fireplace against the front wall. Bobby was talking to Donald but Herbie didn't pay attention. He let his mind wander, thought of the routine of his father coming home in the late afternoon, washing up outside at the hose bib on the side of the house, his heavy footsteps eventually making their way through the kitchen.

The warmth from the fireplace lulled him, made it easy for a blanket of melancholy to descend upon him. He worried, for a moment, about Ellie, hiding in the attic, her father not coming home to her, stuck alone now with their raging mother.

Maybe Grandmother had come by and quieted her by now, had stopped her loud lamentations. Yes. Lamentations.

Like the ones Mother was always reading about in the Bible—cries and lamentations. The beating of the breasts, which must hurt, the gnashing of teeth, the wailing outside in the darkness to rip your soul from your body and then to send it to be consumed in hellfires.

Herbie's world tucked itself inside itself and the evening drew itself together. When the morning came, he would remember the Gillespies sitting down to eat and he and his brothers joining them, mimicking the seemingly formal way they ate their food, using the big spoons to eat their soup, and chattering away—so unlike the hard-baked silence at the dinner table at their own house.

He remembered the warmth from the fireplace in the parlor, the sleepiness, the blankets and pillows pulled from closets, and then the camping out he and his brothers did in the snug parlor. He remembered nothing of the night except the warmth of the house and the blanket he pulled up to his chin.

Mr. Gillespie got up early, ate the breakfast Mrs. Gillespie prepared for him, picked up his metal lunchbox, and went off to the mine. Herbie could hear their movements through the crack the parlor door was left open. He pretended to be asleep, listening to his brothers breathing regularly, Donald occasionally wheezing as though he had a cold.

When Rudy woke, the three sat together in the now-chilly parlor until Mrs. Gillespie came to get them for breakfast. She told them they could return that evening for dinner and a place to sleep if they needed it. She asked to be remembered to their mother.

Bobby came downstairs with a bang, wolfed down some cereal, and left for school.

Donald, Herbie, and Rudy thanked Mrs. Gillespie for her hospitality and ran down the street to their own house.

They stood out front, on the street, looking at its gray bulk, as though they were visitors from out of town, seeing the grim house for the first time. Herbie looked to the attic windows but did not see Ellie. The front door looked like a cruel mouth.

All of them were reluctant to go inside for fear of what condition they might find their mother in. Donald nudged Herbie toward the walkway on the side of the house. Herbie shrugged and began schlepping along, pretending nonchalance. Donald brought up the rear, occasionally giving Rudy a push between the shoulder blades. Rudy growled at Donald.

When Herbie came opposite the hose bib and the aluminum box that held the rough Lava Soap their father used to clean off before he came into the house, he touched the bib tentatively, as though it was a snake, alive and ready to strike. Donald knocked his hand away. "Come on," he said, pushing Herbie forward.

The back door at the top of the steps was unlocked, as usual. Herbie went in through the cold kitchen, past the perpetually locked cellar door. There was no sound other than the ticking of the kitchen clock: 7:47. "I guess we ain't goin' to school today," Herbie said as he slowly moved toward the front of the house.

The door to the parlor was closed, as was the door to their parents' bedroom. Herbie stopped and put his finger to his lips, shushing his brothers, hoping to hear some sound of life—hopefully from Ellie. But there was nothing. Dark drapes hung slovenly from their hangers, covering the windows, damning the faint fall light from outside. Herbie began to think to himself that it looked like he imagined the inside of a tomb to look, but quickly rejected the simile.

Hearing that the coast was clear, Donald raced up the stairs to his bedroom. He flung open the door and threw himself down on his unmade bed.

Rudy, a disciple of his oldest brother, followed, scooted off to his own room, pulled on a sweater against what seemed to be a house with the heat turned off, and lay back on his bed.

Herbie didn't move from the center of the hall. He hoped to yet hear a sound from the attic, a sound to indicate that Ellie was still there. She must be hungry by now, and scared. Herbie sometimes thought of her as an animal—a particularly skittish animal, a rabbit, maybe. He didn't understand her, and understood even less the antipathy their mother had toward the poor girl.

Their mother never had a good word for Ellie. Ellie's whole world was wrapped up in reading books and waiting for their father to come home from work. She went outside only when she was required to—to go to school, or to visit their grandmother, or to run to the store for something their mother forgot to order.

Herbie strained to hear her, but there was nothing— nothing from upstairs except the occasional sound from one of his brothers as one or the other changed his position on the bed.

Herbie knew why their parents' bedroom door was closed. It was always closed. But the door to the parlor was usually left at least partway open. He walked across the hall and grasped the doorknob. When he turned it, it clicked agreeably. He pushed the door open but had to wait for his eyes to adjust to the gloom. All the shades were pulled tightly closed and the only light was the dim ray that came in from the hallway behind him.

Someone had moved the furniture around, clearing away a large space in the middle of the room. There they had set up a pair of strong sawhorses and, on top of them, a plain black coffin.

A red cloth table skirt had been draped over the lower half of the coffin as though someone, intending to secure the skirt around the bottom of the coffin, had been interrupted. The lid to the coffin was up, but from the door Herbie could not see into it. It was too high on the sawhorses.

Still holding tightly to the doorknob, Herbie scanned the dark room, as though expecting that someone might jump out from behind one of the drapes, a maneuver Rudy occasionally pulled when their parents weren't at home and they roamed every nook and cranny of the house except the attic, the cellar, and their parents' bedroom.

The sound of a car passing in the street seeped in through the thick, dark drapes. From the intensity of the light leaking in from behind him, Herbie concluded that the sun had come out and that the chilly day would quickly warm up. That fact gave him an option to move further into the parlor. He could turn around, gather his brothers together, go outside, and maul the mountainside like they usually did on a free day. No school today, no reason to stay indoors, nobody to stop them.

But that seemed too far down Herbie's priority list to consider. Their father had died—at the mines . . . in the mine. And now he was in the parlor, not reading his newspaper, not listening to Mother drone on reading

Scripture, not smoking his pipe, not trying to be funny—to make his brood laugh, while their Mother tried to freeze him with a fierce stare or a tap-tap of her foot.

Father tried to be funny. He wasn't. Now, Herbie realized, there would be no more opportunities to pretend that he'd been funny, to encourage him to serve as a warming balm against Mother's deep freeze.

Someone upstairs dropped something heavy on the floor—followed by a laugh. Herbie was certain it wasn't Ellie. God knows what Ellie was doing in the attic.

Releasing the doorknob as though releasing the tether line to a space capsule, Herbie made up his mind that if this was the last time he'd see his father, he wanted to see him alone, without the attendant underwater-like pallor of the usual wake. He'd been to three wakes in his life, and in each case he couldn't wait to escape. People, mostly old people, sat around talking in low voices as though they were afraid if they spoke in normal volumes they'd wake the dead. Herbie came to the conclusion that's where the term wake came from. You didn't want to wake the dead.

His father even said it when he and Donald and Rudy would get each other going. "Quiet, or you'll wake the dead," their father would say, slightly nodding his head at their mother and smiling.

From the devotionals they were all required to suffer through each night in this very room, Herbie knew exactly where the boards lay that squeaked and groaned. He tiptoed over and around them until he was in front of the coffin. This proximity brought his head above the edge of the lushly polished wooden coffin. He looked in, the muscle springs in his legs ready to affect his escape should anything be amiss.

But nothing was. Their father looked like he was asleep, like he was sometimes in the middle of a summer Sunday—when he lay down on the little patch of grass out back that the boys had failed to kill and napped for an hour or more. The only thing missing was the regular rattle of his breathing from the coal dust stuck to the inside of his lungs. He made no sound now, but the house did. A floorboard on the second floor squeaked then settled.

He felt uneasy staring at his quiet father this way, as though there were some prescribed way he should feel while parked in front of what was the husk of the man he'd known his whole life. The emotions of dealing with a recently dead relative had not yet kicked in. The enormity of the vacuum his father's death had made in their lives was unappreciated by someone of Herbie's age. Not even a full day had passed since his father had left, and although he knew his father's body was now merely a corpse, even that reality had not yet set in.

Herbie placed his hands on the edge of the coffin. The lower half was closed, the table skirt draped around it. The inside of the coffin was luxurious in a plain way—luxurious relative to the style which Herbie and his family were used to.

His father's hands were crossed over his chest, his left hand atop the right, his only jewelry his tarnished wedding ring. He was dressed in his Sunday suit, but it didn't seem to fit him as well as it did when he was alive, as though some of the spirit that had been his father had fled or been deflated. His bear-like presence seemed to have been stuffed with straw.

Herbie looked at his father's face. It seemed crooked, as though he'd forgotten to straighten it when he put it on the morning before. Because of the difficulty of removing the inky coal dust from his eyelashes, they looked as though they had been heightened by mascara. The rest of his face had been scrubbed free of coal dirt, the way it usually was by church on Sunday when his father had had Saturday afternoon off to more thoroughly clean up the everywhere dust.

Something was wrong, though—besides the lopsided look of his father's face. At first he couldn't identify what it was, but when he gently rubbed the back of his hand along his father's cheek, he noticed the beard stubble. Dressed in his Sunday suit, their father should not have stubble on his face. He never did on Sundays. This wasn't Sunday, no. But with the suit went a smooth shave.

Without a second's thought until he stood in front of his parents' closed bedroom door, Herbie knew what he had to do. He stopped, held his breath, and listened like a radar station. He heard someone a few houses away call to someone else and he heard the muffled voices of his brothers upstairs in their bedrooms.

Certain he was safe, he turned the doorknob and entered his parents' bedroom. A weak light burned on one of the nightstands. It dumbly threw a touch of light onto the huge, ornate bed that was covered in a richly patterned duvet. The wallpaper was Victorian, elaborate in its scenes of palatial excess—vertical, patterned, purple stripes three-inches wide dividing the scenes. Fox hunting, a garden party in front of a three-story mansion, a tea party in an enormous parlor with over-stuffed furniture—all lost on Herbie.

Off to the left was what he was looking for—the door to his parents' bathroom.

He hurried in, ignored the claw-footed tub with the scarlet curtains, and went directly to the elaborately decorated medicine cabinet. The contrast between the ornate bedroom and the rest of the house never fazed him; this was just how things were. He swung the mirror away from the medicine chest and groped in the half-darkness for the safety razor and the cup of shaving soap. He briefly ran the tap in the sink to get some water into the shaving soap cup.

Once, when their mother was away with Ellie visiting at their grandmother's, their father had come into the dining room with his face covered with shaving soap, mixing the soap in the cup with the short-bristled brush. "All right, young man," he said to Donald. "Sit yerself down here"—he pointed with the razor in his other hand at one of the dining room chairs—"and get them whiskers off yer face." Donald had obliged, sitting up straight and proper for once in his life.

Their father set the cup on the edge of the dining room table, then twisted the bottom of the shaft of the safety razor. When the top of it opened like a metal flower in fast-motion, he extracted the double-edge blade, and made a "Haaaarrrruuuummmmmppp" sound as though he were about to embark on an unpleasant task.

He closed the razor, put the double-edge blade carefully down on the table, and began stirring up the soap in the cup. With the brush, he began painting soap on Donald's cheeks and neck. "Ya shouldn't let them whiskers get this unruly," he said, making great huffing and puffing sounds as though he were a barber who was very displeased. "Now . . . put yer head back so's I kin slit yer neck ear to ear." He laughed like a pirate. Donald began laughing and couldn't stop.

His father began meticulously "shaving" Donald's face, making great elaborate strokes with the razor as though he were scything vast acres of wheat. Donald laughed so much his nose began to run. "Ah," the barber said, "we have a bleeder here!" Rudy began running around the room, squealing in unadulterated and uncontrolled delight. Herbie pressed his fist to his mouth in a futile attempt to stifle his unique chortling style of laughter.

When their father finished, he pulled a damp wash rag from his back pocket and wiped it all over Donald's face as though he were trying to smother him. It barely stifled Donald's laughter. He stepped back, considering the quality of his work, and made a deep bow. When he came back up, he said, "That'll be four bits, kid."

"Take it out of my allowance," Donald managed to get out before he again doubled over with laughter.

Turning quickly on his heel, their father marched back into the bedroom with the cup of soap and the razor blade. He came out ten minutes later looking fresh and revived, except for the telltale mascara-like highlighting to his eyes, his perpetual beauty accessory from the fine dust of the coal mines.

"You keep this between us," he commanded the boys. "I think it would break your mother's heart to realize that you fellers are growing up and'll be shaving soon and goin' into the world on yer own. She dreams of keepin' all of ya like ya are right now."

Herbie's mind played the scene over twice before he stood looking down at his father's face. He set the razor carefully on the edge of the coffin, pulled a heavy chair over, knelt on it, and began stirring up a soap lather with the brush. Carefully, gently, he began applying soap to his father's pale face.

He pressed the razor gently against his father's right cheek, just at the edge of the sideburn, and skated it along his father's jawbone. The razor left a clean lane the way a snowplow did in the middle of a snowstorm. Herbie regarded his handiwork in the weak light from the doorway and was satisfied.

But the stroke left him with a problem. The razor was clotted with soap and little whiskers and he'd forgotten to bring along a wet cloth onto which he could wipe the mess. He backed off the chair and walked back to his parents' bathroom to rinse off the razor and to moisten a towel. The running water hid the sound of the back door opening and the sounds of footsteps coming through the kitchen and dining room.

When he came out of the bedroom, razor in one hand and damp towel in the other, he ran directly into the tall, thin, black-clad bat-like creature that was his mother. Without a second's hesitation, she slapped him across his face.

The attack came so suddenly that Herbie had no time to react. The force of the blow sent a sparkling nighttime veil over his brain for a moment. He dropped the razor. "You little bastard!" his mother hissed. "Desecrating the body of your dead father!"

Herbie stood stunned and dumb. "But . . ." he managed to say before her other hand came around and slapped the other side of his face. "You monster," she spat, raising her arm for another slap.

The next slap never came. Another tall, thin, black-clad figure behind her—his grandmother—moved forward a step and grabbed her daughter's wrist in a gnarled talon. "Stop," she said simply, still grasping his mother's wrist.

His mother swung around, as though to slap her own mother, but before she could, Herbie's grandmother grasped her free wrist and held it firmly. "Enough."

For a long moment the world stopped in its orbit. Nothing moved, not even the hearts of the three.

Then Herbie's mother shattered the tableaux. "You little bastards," she said. "If it weren't for you I wouldn't be in this mess."

Herbie intuited that she wasn't speaking only of his dead father, but of her whole life. And in an instant he realized that his mother's constant angry edge was in part his making. He and Donald and Rudy and Ellie were responsible for her situation in life, for her perpetual misery. He felt shaken and hollow—and resentful.

"I didn't ask to be born" nearly came to his lips, but the sad look on his grandmother's face stopped him. At that moment, she released her daughter, who seemed to anticipate the moment, as she rushed into the bedroom, pushing Herbie out of her way—pushing him hard against the edge of the doorway.

His grandmother reached for him, steadied him before he could stumble, pulled him toward her, and pulled the bedroom door closed. Her grip on his wrist was as hard as her grip had been on his mother. Like a black scarecrow come to life, she led him out of the room. She nodded toward the coffin, where the shaving soap made his father look like Santa Claus.

"That's the job of the undertaker," she said simply, directing him, with her gaze, upstairs.

"He should have shaved father before he put his clothes on," Herbie said, not sure where the courage came from to talk back to his grandmother. She was the only human being in the world even his mother feared.

His grandmother stood motionless, her last gesture directing him upstairs frozen on her.

Herbie turned and began to slowly ascend the steps. "Shoulda done it before," he muttered under his breath. "Shoulda, coulda, woulda," he added, repeating the favorite refrain of Butch Kadinski, one of his only school friends.

The commotion downstairs had alerted Donald and Rudy and they peered out from Donald's doorway. Donald's left eyebrow raised in a question mark.

"They didn't shave father before they brought him home," Herbie said before closing his bedroom door behind him. He dropped onto his unmade bed and laced his fingers behind his head, looking at the ceiling as though he were going to torch the wallpaper with his fiery stare. He felt like crying but didn't think he had the energy. He slapped himself across the face with his right hand to feel again what it felt like when his mother struck him. It stung, and then the sting went away. He felt his heartbeat slow and felt the room begin to cool.

His brothers were whispering in Donald's room. He could hear his grandmother moving around downstairs; it sounded as though she was moving furniture. He thought he should go help but didn't want to get right back into the middle of woman rage.

He didn't know how long he lay there because there was no window in his bedroom—like there was in Donald's.

Maybe he dozed; maybe he thought he did. He began to hear people moving around downstairs. Several times the front door opened, so it must have been something important that was happening. There was the sound of more furniture being manhandled.

The only times there was this much sound in the old house was when he and his brothers made it. And sometimes they did that just to chase away the intimidating silence—the silence their mother brewed.

He turned his head away from the door and tried to nap, but he couldn't. Before he decided finally that he could not manufacture a nap, the door to his bedroom opened quietly and Ellie sat down on the edge of his bed. He turned to look at her. She wore a shapeless calico dress that was too big for her. Her eyes peered out of skin that looked spectral. Her mouth was pressed tightly together so it looked like a pencil line drawn on a tablet.

"Whazzup?" he said quietly, not wanting to frighten her. He and his brothers felt that one of their jobs in life was to make sure that Ellie knew to be apprehensive when they were around; that way she'd grow up to be wary of guys. He'd been feeling lately that maybe they were doing their job a bit too well.

Ellie didn't answer him. She just sat there, playing with her hands.

"Father is dead," Herbie finally said. "I saw him down-stairs."

Ellie nodded as though she knew all about it, which she probably did. She glanced out the door in the direction of downstairs but she didn't make a move toward the door.

"The bastards at the undertaker place didn't even shave

him good," Herbie said. Ellie didn't wince at the word bastard. Their mother frequently used the word to describe their father and the boys.

Ellie continued to sit quietly, her hands like two spiders feeling around each other for an opening.

Herbie sat up, fluffed his pillow behind him, and said, "Are you hungry?"

She shook her head.

"Did you get something to eat?"

She nodded.

Suddenly, for no apparent reason, Ellie bolted. She was out the door and quietly sprinting down the hall before Herbie could catch his breath.

He imagined that he watched her float up the stairs to the attic—the stairs drawing themselves up behind her like a fist closing.

Then he heard the sound. Someone was slowly making their way up the stairs from the first floor. The steps spoke of weariness and resolve. It had to be their grandmother; their mother knew which sides of the steps to avoid to fake out the creakiness of the old staircase.

When the footsteps reached the top of the landing, they headed toward Donald's room. It was their grandmother. He could just make out her voice as it bounced from inside Donald's room, down the hall, and into his. "You boys get dressed now," she said. "People will be coming by soon to say goodbye to your father, and as the men of the house you need to be there." Herbie thought he caught the sound of a weary sigh.

"Put on your Sunday suits; then come downstairs."

Herbie had risen from his bed, and he stood in the doorway to his bedroom. He could see his grandmother's tall straight black-clad back framed in Donald's doorway. "That means you, too, Herbert," she said without turning to look at him.

"Yes, ma'am," Herbie said without thinking. He turned back into his bedroom, walked to the clothes closet, opened it, and pulled out what a year earlier had been Donald's Sunday suit. He was still a size smaller than Donald was then, so the suit hung loosely on him. He began to change his clothes, shrugging himself into the dead-leaf brown two-piece suit over a plain white shirt with a loosened already-tied tie with a painting of an at-attention hunting dog on it.

He pulled the tie tight like a noose, moved it around until it felt right, then schlepped out of his room down to Donald's. Donald was slowly pulling himself together, and Rudy was down the hall in his little bedroom getting himself ready. Halfway dressed, Donald came over to Herbie and flipped down the left side of his shirt collar. "Don't look like a doofus," Donald said. "And don't act like one, either."

Donald seemed very mature all of a sudden. He wasn't even mumbling about getting dressed up like he did every Sunday morning.

Rudy came running down the hall, his shirttail hanging out, a tie in his hand, his suit jacket trailing behind him. Herbie remembered the suit well; it had been three years since he'd been small enough to wear it. It was light tan and lightweight and made Rudy look like the nougat in a Three Musketeers bar.

When they were sufficiently ready, the three of them stood at the top of the staircase, none of them eager to be the first to descend into the pool of low murmur that broiled below. Herbie glanced down the hall at the recessed ladder to the attic. There was no evidence of Ellie, and he was sure there wouldn't be. No one was strong or foolish enough to go hunting her up so they could force her to come downstairs.

"You're the oldest," Herbie finally said, giving Donald a push toward the stairs.

Donald descended the stairs slowly, as though he were going to a funeral. That was the thought that passed across Herbie's brain at that moment; he wanted to laugh at his own cluelessness—but refused.

They followed the murmuring to the parlor where folding chairs had been set up in rows. Ladies from the neighborhood sat bent into each other whispering while others stood in small groups talking solemnly. Their mother sat in one of the big stuffed parlor chairs off to one side, while their grandmother stood like a dark steeple beside her. The younger widow was sobbing while her mother remained passive and impervious. They were both dressed in black. So were most of the local ladies—except for Mrs. Hefferling, who wore an extremely dark red dress the color of dried blood, and Mrs. Berashki, who hadn't taken off her dark green cloth coat.

Against the front wall of the big room, the coffin reigned—a large flower arrangement on either side, the table skirts attached and dignified. (The coffin was still high enough that all Herbie could see of their father from where he stood was the tip of his nose.)

With this many people in the parlor and with the furniture moved around, the usually big room seemed close and confining. The front door opened slowly, then the vestibule door, and a black-clad woman Herbie did not recognize entered, walked around the chairs, went up the aisle in the middle, knelt in front of the coffin, crossed herself, muttered a prayer, and rose to approach and whisper to his mother, then his grandmother.

The air in the room felt stale and thicker than real air, as though it had been pumped in especially for the wake.

Before their mother could notice them and tell them what to do, Herbie slipped out through the dining room where a single lady sat on one of the chairs with her head in her hands. There was food in dishes covering most of the table. The door to the kitchen was closed, but Herbie could hear male voices coming from the other side.

He pushed open the door to the kitchen, which was crowded with neighborhood men Herbie knew either by name or by sight. They were drinking wine and beer and talking in hushed voices. They all wore their Sunday suits except for Mr. Schmidt, who didn't own one—and who was the town atheist, so didn't need a Sunday suit. He was mixing himself a highball from bottles sitting beside the sink.

Mr. Gillespie noticed Herbie and moved over to encourage him to come in. "Ya want a highball, or is it too early in the day?" Mr. Gillespie asked, winking at him. Herbie smiled—then nodded. Mr. Gillespie laughed and nudged him across the room to a safe place near the back door.

Herbie felt better here, among the gruff, scarred men with the black deep-earth eye shadow. They felt like a cage of various-sized bears, nudging each other, bumping about. Their occasional laughter should have cut like a sharp insult to his dead father, but it wasn't like that at all.

They all knew what they knew about the mines; they'd been to wakes before. His father had taken him to the wake of an Irish miner named Kevin O'Grady, a tall gaunt man.

As the wake moved along, the men removed Mr. O'Grady from the coffin, stood him up in a corner, and put a drink in his hand. "There now," one of the men said. "There's the Kevin O'Grady we all remember." Everyone laughed.

Raised under his mother's heavy church influence, and with her permissiveness in all other things, Herbie was torn between feeling outraged and comforted by the rough camaraderie of Mr. O'Grady's friends.

He never told his mother about Mr. O'Grady. He already knew what she'd say in her dismissive way. "Those vile Catholics!"

He hoped the men here would stand his father up in the corner. That would drive his mother batshit—looney enough that grandmother would be unable to control her, and then there'd be hell to pay.

From somewhere in the crowd, someone—Mr. Gillespie?—pushed a little glass of wine into Herbie's hand. He'd had wine before. One Sunday night, their mother had insisted that their father put together the devotional for the family. He'd talked about the Wedding Feast at Canaan and the changing of water into wine. Mother didn't approve of drinking, so he emphasized that the first miracle Jesus performed was to confirm the sanctity of marriage.

After she went to bed, though, he'd gone into the kitchen, reached high up to the top shelf, and brought down a tall thin bottle of Manachevitz fruit wine. Herbie didn't remember what kind of fruit it was, but it was thick and sweet, better than cherry soda. Father had given each of them a little glass, held his up in salute, and told them to sip their wine slowly. Donald drank his down dutifully and Rudy made a face like it was castor oil or something.

"The fact that Jesus turned water into wine as his first miracle on this Earth means that Jesus approved of wine," their father said. When they were finished, he carefully washed and dried the little glasses and replaced what was left of the bottle so it was out of reach and out of their mother's sight.

Herbie thought of that as he sipped his sweet wine in the little space between the kitchen and the back door, the little space they used as an open clothes closet. Occasionally, a man pushed his way past Herbie to go outside to have a smoke, while another worked his way back in. When the back door opened, cold air rushed in, pushed by a breeze that carried smells of winter with it. The aroma of warm fireplaces came with it, too, but Herbie wasn't cold. The warmth thrown off by the shifting menagerie of men pushed against the cold air trying to intrude.

Outside, the light was failing. There was an orange glow as the sun dropped toward dusk. Herbie calculated that there were now more people in their house than had ever been in it in total since he'd been born. It made the house feel at once warm and alien.

And suddenly he didn't want to be there. He put the empty glass on the kitchen counter, and when the next neighbor man went outside to smoke, Herbie fell into his wake and slipped outside.

The chilly air bit at him as he skulked through the half-dozen men smoking unfiltered cigarettes in the small backyard. He went down the back steps as silent as a cat, took the left turn around the side of the house, and was gone into the dark patches in the street outside the weak influence of the streetlights planted every fifty yards.

He crossed the street and headed uphill. Two trains, on opposite sides of the river, wailed like banshees as they raced through town, one rattling along hauling boxcars, the other click-clicking over the rail joints with a half-mile line of empty coal cars.

Herbie knew the path well. He and Donald and Rudy spent nearly every afternoon up here, after school, unless it was raining, when they terrorized the floors and walls of their house. The well-worn trail angled upwards toward Big Rock on the top of Bear Mountain, grooved by generations of kids, going nearly straight up instead of switchbacking like the adult walking paths did.

His breathing came rapidly until he told himself to slow down, to control himself. His breathing came rapidly, too, because of the cold. He should have checked the air temperature and dressed accordingly, not headed out in his stupid hand-me-down Sunday suit. And his shoes—they were the dumb Sunday shoes with smooth soles that didn't get a good grip. He slipped and slid over the rocky outcroppings, but he knew the lower part of the path well enough that even if he fell, he was sure he could catch himself before he really hurt anything.

After a few minutes of senseless rushing, he slowed down to a fast walk. By the half-moon, he could make out the silhouettes of protruding rocks. He slowed further as he passed into the solid shadow under trees filled with dead but still clinging leaves.

A moment later, in a clearing, he stopped to look behind him, to make sure he was not being followed. There were lights on in most of the houses clinging to the side of the mountain. The dim lights in his house escaped only thinly around the thick dark drapes that kept the inside of the house cave-like. He could make out the bare light that was around the back of the house above the back door, where the men were smoking and talking in low voices.

Somewhere a cat shrieked and the breeze increased its velocity so that he turned up the collar of his suit jacket and wrestled with buttoning the top button which had never been used. His breath floated in front of his face like a fog. He gritted his teeth and continued upward, his motivation uncertain, his destination a little cave two-thirds of the way up the mountain, a little clubhouse dug under a huge conglomerate rock about half the size of Big Rock.

He'd be safe there, away from whatever would be coming from their mother now that their father was gone. Donald sensed what was coming, Rudy was too young and dumb to know, but their lives were now forever changed and would never again be nearly as okay as they had been. He knew their mother. This would be just what she needed to stay in her bedroom all day, every day, to beat at them with her wailing and moaning and her bitterness. Even their grandmother would have no power over her, now that she held the hammer of a dead husband. It had worked for his grandmother; it would work for his mother.

Herbie felt the soft tatters of childhood slip away from him, the hardening carapace of adulthood encasing him like a cold shroud. For the moment, the chilly breeze failed to affect him. There were colder things to consider. But the cold kept reminding him of itself.

He hugged himself, to try to get warm, and resumed his climb.

In ten minutes he was at the mouth of their cave. Donald called it the Bat Cave because he read too many comic books, so of course Rudy called it the Bat Cave, too. Herbie referred to it merely as "home." He lowered his head and entered, the leaves on the floor cushioning his steps. He moved deeper into the darkness, reaching out to follow the contours of the right wall with his hand until it reached familiar outcroppings.

His feet crossed from leaves onto a dirt surface and he knew he was near the fire ring, the little circle of stones they'd erected to contain their campfires. His toe encountered the edge of the ring and he ran his hand along the wall again, looking for the loose rock, as big as a brick. He lifted it from the little ledge on which it rested, and from beneath pulled out half a book of matches with an ad for Charles Atlas on it and a mail-in coupon printed on the inside.

He knelt down expertly and struck a match, moving it quickly under the crumpled newspaper at the bottom of the ring. The paper caught fire cheerfully, flickering to life like a little god. The orange flame quickly grew to kiss the pile of broken twigs above it, investing them with life; they in turn caressed the small dead tree branches above them, warming them, coaxing them to join the fun. Herbie smiled, the first hint of warmth filling his blood with calm.

Both Herbie and Donald were still in that stage of boyhood where they could accurately be called pyromaniacs—slaves to the god of fire in both its concept and reality. On the hottest days, they still built a fire in their cave. It was a sacrament—an offering that must be made.

Herbie pulled an old wooden candle box forward and set it intimately close to the little fire. He sat down and rubbed his hands before him, letting the fire warm them. He had no fear that anyone would ever see the fire. The lip of the cave rose like a pout, cutting off the fire to people below him; and it was back far enough into the cave that even people driving along Highway 903 across the river, by the abandoned uranium mines, wouldn't spot it, because they didn't have an angle on it.

Except for Donald and Rudy, nobody knew where he was likely to be, and nobody knew he had his very own fire. The breeze moved by outside the cave but it did not penetrate. He was safe—like the "wild Indians" his mother called them. He often daydreamed of the Leni Lenape Indians who had once roamed these mountains, sitting around campfires at night, roasting venison, telling stories about the spirits that accompanied them through life—and beyond.

He wished that the God his mother made them pray to would allow his father to come by to visit with him, even if only for a moment, on his way to Heaven. Just for a few moments. So they could talk. Or just sit listening to the night sounds. For a last visit, but this time alone, without all the other people in the house soaking him up, what there was left of him after work and mother got finished with him.

He got up, moved back into the very depths of the cave, and came back with the threadbare little Army blanket his father had used in World War II. He wrapped himself in it like a shawl.

Outside the cave, the half-moon lit up the sky, whose clouds had all blown through. Without the clouds to hold some of the day's warmth to the Earth, it would be one frosty night ahead. Herbie laid increasingly larger pieces of branches on the fire, where they happily joined the conflagration, the warmth spreading throughout Herbie's underworld.

Outside the cave mouth, in the sky, there was a sudden rush. Herbie started, but a second later relaxed as the dark wings of an owl circled past. Maybe that was father's soul leaving his earthly body, his soul a night bird heading away to Heaven. Herbie smiled and used a long, sharp stick to move around some of the burning branches. The fire crackled and chirped merrily.

Herbie's face began to feel warm, his knees, too. Once the campfire began generating this much heat, Herbie usually thought of what Donald had told him. The planet Mercury, the planet closest to the sun, gets extremely hot on the half of the planet facing the sun and very cold on the half facing away; Herbie's body felt like that on a cold night in front of the campfire. Eventually he would have to get up and turn around, warm his backside, and let his front settle back down.

He heard the owl cry out, farther up the mountainside, and then he heard another sound—some rocks being scattered. Before he could get up to see if it was a stray dog or a bear, a figure appeared in the cave entrance. It took him a moment to realize that it was Ellie, bundled up in a winter coat with a woolen hat pulled down over her head. "Wha—? What are you doin' here?" he managed.

"Don't be mad," she started as she moved slowly into the firelight. The pockets of her coat were bulging like the cheeks of a chipmunk.

Herbie stood up, the long straight stick still in his hand. "I ain't mad," he said. "Just surprised." He tossed the stick toward the back of the cave, suddenly afraid she would think he was going to use it to hurt her.

She walked up to the fire and bent down to warm her bare hands. She made a soft murmuring sound back in her throat. "It's cold," she said.

"And it's gonna get a lot colder before it gets warmer," Herbie said. "A lot colder." He sat down on one end of the candle box and patted his hand on the other. "Sit down and get warm," he said. She walked over tentatively.

"I ain't gonna bite you, ya know," he said.

She sat and gazed into the fire.

"What's in the pockets?" Herbie finally asked.

"Sandwiches," she said. "Father always saved half of his sandwich for me. We'll need to eat." She pulled out half of a sandwich wrapped in wax paper. "Summer sausage, orange cheese, French's yellow mustard, oleomargarine, and white bread," she said. "Always the same."

Herbie accepted the sandwich, opened it, and took a bite. It tasted stale, but he was hungry. And besides, it had spent a whole day in a lunchbox down in the bottom of a mine pit. It ought to be a little stale.

"They'll never find us here," Ellie said. "This is a good hideout."

Just then, there was more rattling of stones outside the cave mouth.

Herbie jumped to his feet and retrieved the long straight stick. Ellie ran—bent over in a defensive stance—to the back of the cave.

"Herbie," someone called from outside the cave. "It's us." Herbie dropped the stick and ran to the front of the cave. In the silver moonlight, Donald and Rudy were struggling up the rocks, each carrying two grocery bags. Herbie ran down to take one from Rudy. He hefted the bag—at least fifteen pounds. The kid was tougher than he thought.

The three of them lurched to the cave mouth. Inside, Ellie stood behind the fire, lit in golden flickering light.

What the—?" Donald said. "How'd you get here?" He set the bags down on a flat rock. "How'd you know where here was?"

"Yeah," Rudy added. "This place is secret—top secret."

Ellie backed up a step, assaulted by their questioning.

"I know a lot of things," she whispered.

Herbie stepped forward, taking Rudy's second bag from him and depositing it in the back of the cave with their cache of Spam and crackers and soda. "She knows lots of stuff," he said—not sure what those things were, but confident in knowing that he'd never heard her tell a lie, so what she said must be true.

He picked up two more thick branches and put them on the fire; the fire accepted them greedily and made them its own. "Let's get comfy," Herbie said, retaking his seat on the one side of the candle box, motioning Ellie to come back over and join him. She did. He put his arm around her.

Donald and Rudy took seats on a flat rock on the other side of the fire. "Things are getting ugly down there," Donald said. "Some of the men in the kitchen were laughing, you know, like to hide what they thought, and mother heard them and went nuts."

"Yeah," Rudy said. "She went bonkers. Screaming, throwing things. A real nutter."

"Everybody left. Then she started yelling at Grandmother," Donald said. "So when Grandmother steered her into the bedroom, we scatted." He pointed his right thumb at the grocery bags. "We already had this stuff salted away in the shed out back."

"We're here for good now," Rudy said, as though it was something he'd wanted to do all his life. "Yessirree, I ain't never goin' back there. She'd kill us." He leaned back on his elbows, gazing at the fire, opening the top buttons of his heavy jacket as the fire warmed him.

"We got enough stuff to stay about a year," Donald said as he unbuttoned the top two buttons on his coat. "They'll never find us."

"I'm stayin', too," Ellie said.

Donald shook his head. "For tonight, maybe, but tomorrow we gotta get you back down the hill and outta town." He removed his wool hat and scratched his head. "I think we have an aunt and uncle in Philadelphia. You can stay there." His word seemed to be final.

Ellie shook her head. "I'm stayin' right here . . . with youse guys."

"No way," Donald said. "You're a girl. Girls don't make good cave dwellers."

"Maybe, maybe not," Herbie said. "Girls and women used to take care of the caves while the cavemen went out and killed dinosaurs that the cavewomen could cook up."

"Yeah," Rudy said. "I heard about that."

"No girls," Donald said. "They're trouble."

"I ain't leavin'," Ellie said. "And if you pull me out of here and take me back, I'll tell mother and everyone else where you're hiding." She crossed her arms over her chest and stuck out her tongue.

Herbie laughed. "She's got us there." He gently patted Ellie on the back. "You kin stay." He waved his free hand around the cave. "Hell. We're the only family we've got left."

"Our aunt and uncle . . . " Donald began, then stopped.

Ellie leaned into Herbie's side. "When it's time to go to bed, will you tell me a story?"

"Sure," Herbie said. "We'll all take turns, until we run out." He felt expansive at the moment.

"Then we'll make some up," Rudy said, yawning. "I'm hungry."

Ellie reached into her pocket and tossed him a half-sandwich over the top of the flames. He caught it easily. He unfolded the wax paper and examined the inside of the sandwich and stuck the end into his mouth. "One time there was this giant wild killer gorilla," he said between bites. "And it was running all over the hills, trying to catch and eat people."

Ellie burrowed deeper into Herbie's sleeve.

"He lived in a cave on the mountainside. In fact, it was this very cave. We know that because when we first found this cave, we found people bones in here. Ain't that right, guys?"

Donald smiled. "Oh yeah——"

Ellie smiled and, within the minute, was safely asleep.